Sorority Girl

By
John Locke

SORORITY GIRL

Cover Designed by: Claudia Jackson
Copyright © iStock_34826070

Published by John Locke Books, LLC

Visit the author's website:
http://www.donovancreed.com

ISBN 978-1-937656-08-9 (eBook)
ISBN 978-1-937656-09-6 (Paperback)

Version 2016.11.08

Medical Warning:

Talk to your doctor before beginning a John Locke series, as studies have shown them to be habit-forming and highly addictive. Do not read Locke if you suffer from high blood pressure or other heart-related issues, as readers often experience mood swings, increased pulses, elevated heart rates, and have reported unexpected shifts in body position that take them to the edge of their seats. Do not drive or use machinery while reading Locke novels.

Locke novels are not for everyone, and may cause serious reactions including insomnia, night terrors, and uncontrollable, maniacal laughter. Tell your doctor right away if you have these, or if you experience unusual changes in your behavior including increased sexual urges, palpitations, or prolonged erections. Common side effects include confusion, hysteria, and trouble swallowing a given premise.

Do not drink alcohol while reading Locke novels, though those with a history of drug or alcohol abuse may be more prone to understanding the material. Adverse reactions to Locke novels include nausea and vomiting, loss of appetite, severe itching, rectal bleeding, purple spots under the skin, and Jimmy Legs. In extreme cases, readers have reported laughing so hard they not only shit their pants, but other's pants, as well. Upon completing a Locke series be prepared to experience symptoms of withdrawal, including fear, anger, extreme sadness, and moderate to severe depression.

Ask your doctor today if John Locke novels are right for you!

Personal Message from John Locke:

John Locke

New York Times Best Selling Author

Guinness World Record Holder for eBook Sales!

8th Member of the Kindle Million Sales Club!

(Members include James Patterson, George R.R. Martin, and Lee Child)

John Locke had 4 of the top 10 eBooks on Amazon/Kindle at the same time, including #1 and #2!

...Had 6 of the top 20 books _at the same time_!

...Had 8 books in the top 43 _at the same time_!

...Has written 30 books in five years in _six separate genres_, _All best-sellers_!

...Has been published throughout the world in numerous languages by the world's most prestigious publishing houses!

...Winner, Second Act Magazine's Story of the Year!

...Named by Time Magazine as one of the "Stars of the DIY-Publishing Era"

Wall Street Journal: "John Locke (is) transforming the 'book' business"

John Locke

New York Times Best Selling Author
#1 Best Selling Author on Amazon Kindle

Donovan Creed Series:

Lethal People
Lethal Experiment
Saving Rachel
Now & Then
Wish List
A Girl Like You
Vegas Moon
The Love You Crave
Maybe
Callie's Last Dance
Because We Can!
This Means War!

Emmett Love Series:

Follow the Stone
Don't Poke the Bear
Emmett & Gentry
Goodbye, Enorma
Rag Soup
Spider Rain

Dani Ripper Series:

Call Me!
Promise You Won't Tell?
Teacher, Teacher
Don't Tell Presley!
Abbey Rayne

Dr. Gideon Box Series:

Bad Doctor
Box
Outside the Box
Boxed In!

Other:

Kill Jill
Casting Call
When David Died
Sorority Girl

Kindle Worlds:

A Kiss for Luck (Kindle Only)

Non-Fiction:

How I sold 1 Million eBooks in 5 Months!

Dedication:

To all my friends and family members: Be safe.

There are people in the world who want a piece of you.

Don't make it too easy for them to get it.

Sorority Girl

Chapter 1

IT HAD BEEN building up inside her all day.

Yesterday—a million years ago—daughter Lindy gave her two beautifully-wrapped gifts and a birthday card that made her cry. Today Nancy's fighting the urge to strangle her daughter with her bare hands.

It's always something.

Parenting's a blood sport. A fuse on a powder keg, waiting for a spark.

This time a letter made the difference. A single envelope with a single stamp containing a single paragraph on a single page that informed her parents Lindy failed out of college. According to the letter, she simply stopped showing up for classes.

Nancy called her husband, Ryan, gave him the news. Told him Lindy claimed the whole thing was a mix up, all was fine. But they knew better. Now, 10:35 p.m., Lindy's home, and her parents are having a shit fit. Ryan, reminding his daughter he spent $200,000 on her education. "Not counting that semester in Australia," he adds.

Nancy raises her voice an octave and takes the battle baton from her husband: "Your father's paying $800 a month for the apartment in Dallas you just *had* to have, where you were supposedly going to find a job, and now you can't even *go* there!"

Ryan yells, "Who *says* she can't? It's time to get off her ass. Since she's not going to graduate, she may as well get a job. In Dallas."

"You're kicking me out of the *house?*" Lindy says.

"Call it what you want. this was *your* dream, not ours. *You're* the one who wanted to move to Dallas to live with your friends."

The doorbell rings, but no one moves.

Ryan continues: "Six months ago you handed me a lease, begged me to sign it. So I did. You were supposed to be there by now, getting a job. But here you sit."

Doorbell rings again.

"Are you expecting someone?"

"Kayla said she might stop by."

"It's eleven o'clock."

"Ten-forty-five."

Ryan frowns. As Lindy heads to the door he says, "This discussion isn't over, young lady. Far from it!"

Twelve seconds later Lindy's backing into the den. At first it doesn't register what's happening: three men wearing ski masks, two of them with assault rifles. Nancy screams as the third man—the guy in charge—shoves Lindy onto the couch and growls: "Who else is home?"

Ryan's too startled to speak.

Nancy's begging: "Please! Don't hurt us!"

The guy in charge repeats the question. Ryan says, "No one. It's just us."

"Lying would be a huge mistake. Where's your wallet?"

Ryan retrieves his wallet from his back pocket.

"Toss it," the man says.

Ryan does, then tries to comfort Lindy, who's shaking like a newborn faun. "Shh," he says. "It's going to be all right."

The man takes a moment to study Ryan's driver's license and credit cards. Then says, "Maybe yes, maybe no. Depends on how you act during the next two minutes."

2

Nancy says, "W-we'll do wh-whatever you s-say. Please: take wh-whatever you w-want. Just d-don't hurt us."

He removes his backpack, unzips a section, removes three sets of handcuffs. Tosses the first one to Ryan and says, "Put them on, *Ryan*." When he does, the man looks at Nancy and says, "What's your name?"

"N-Nancy."

He tosses her a set and says, "Put them on, N-Nancy."

The two goons behind him laugh. But it's a menacing laugh, and the sound makes Ryan's blood run cold.

When Nancy's cuffed he throws the third set to Lindy. "What's your name, Sweet Thing?"

"Lindy."

He turns to his men. "Lindy. You like that?"

They do. They like it a lot.

As Lindy starts to put the cuffs on he says, "No. Stand up. Mom and Dad? Move closer together. Lindy? Fasten their cuffs with the ones I gave you." After she does, he says, "Good. Now come here."

"Sir?" Ryan says. "Please. She's just a kid. Don't hurt her. You can have whatever you want."

"What if I want *her*?"

"*No!*" Lindy screams. She starts to run, but the man pivots, dives, catches her arm before she clears the doorway that leads to the kitchen. She yelps in pain as he squeezes her arm and lowers her to the floor. "Face down, Lindy."

"No!" Nancy screams. "Let her *go!*"

She and Ryan get to their feet.

"Shoot them," the man in charge says.

"No!" Lindy yells. "I'll do whatever you want."

He puts his hand up. "What do you mean?"

Lindy turns her body enough to make eye contact. "Please. Don't hurt us."

3

"I understand *that* part. I'm interested in the other thing you said. Say it again."

Her lips are trembling. "I'll...do whatever you want."

"Whatever I want covers a lot of ground, Sweet Thing."

Lindy says nothing.

Ryan says, "We've got cash, jewelry, electronics. Take whatever you want. We won't report it. You have my word."

"You may or may not report it if you live. But you *can't* report it if you're dead."

Nancy's face starts hemorrhaging tears.

"Sir?" Lindy says. "I can show you where the jewelry is."

He looks at Ryan. "Got any guns?"

Ryan pauses.

"Don't lie to me!" the man warns.

"One. A handgun. In the master bedroom."

"I can show you," Lindy says.

"What else can you show me, Sweet Thing?"

Lindy's eyes are brimming with tears.

"I asked you a question," he says.

"I...I'm not sure what you mean."

"You said you'd do whatever I want. Just so you know, I'm fond of pussy."

Lindy's eyes go wide.

"No!" Ryan shouts.

The man takes a step toward Lindy. "Which is it, Sweet Thing? Do I get the *anything* you offered? Or the *no* your father just said? Think carefully before you answer."

Lindy raises herself to a sitting position and starts unbuttoning her blouse.

Chapter 2

"RELAX FOR NOW," the man says. "I was just testing your commitment. When we fuck, you won't be a willing participant. It'll be violent as hell. That, I can promise you."

Though Lindy stops unbuttoning her blouse, her fingers keep trembling.

The man, clearly fixated on her, says, "I like you, Lindy. I truly do."

"Thank you."

"That said, I have a serious character flaw where women are concerned: most can't be trusted. Can you?"

"Yes sir."

"Swear to God?"

She nods.

"Say it."

"I swear to God you can trust me."

"I know your names, understand?"

She nods.

"And I obviously know where you live. You try to burn me, I'll come back and ruin that pretty smile of yours. I'll bust every perfect tooth out of your mouth with the butt of my knife, then use the blade to slice off your nipples. You believe me?"

"Y-Yes sir."

His eyes travel from Ryan to Nancy and back to Lindy. "If I let you live—you'll do what?"

"Anything you say."

He turns to Ryan. "Personally, I believe her."

Ryan says, "You can trust all of us."

"Really? I can trust *all* of you?" He shakes his head. "Here's how I see it: Lindy, yes. You? Maybe. But I can tell you right now, Nancy's not gonna make it."

Nancy starts wailing.

Ryan says, "Look. She's scared to death. Trust me: she's not going to tell anyone."

One of the men says: "This is bullshit. We already agreed: no survivors."

The leader says, "Let's think it through. I tell you to bring guns, and you show up with assault rifles. *Assault* rifles? *Really?* How much *noise* you think you'll make shooting them?"

"My knife's pretty quiet."

"And so is mine. But how about we give Ryan a chance to save his family?" He removes his phone from his pocket and presses a button. "I'm going to ask you some questions and record your answers. Ready?"

Ryan nods.

"Good. We'll start with your full name, date of birth, and social security number."

Ryan gives up the information.

"Now the combination to your safe."

"We don't have a safe."

"Excuse me?"

"There's no safe."

He looks at Lindy.

She shakes her head.

"Well that's disappointing."

He records Nancy's information, then looks at Lindy, but she says nothing.

"It's okay, Sweet Thing. Yours is the least important."

He puts his phone back in his pocket and says, "Lindy? Let's go find the gun, the jewelry, and whatever else we can turn into cash." She stands, he grabs his backpack and follows her to the master bedroom, and confiscates the handgun. Then she opens the dresser drawer where Nancy keeps her jewelry. Surprisingly, the man takes none of it.

"Where's the cash?"

"He doesn't keep cash here."

"I guarantee you he has something somewhere."

She thinks a minute. Then says, "There's a small box in his study."

"Show me."

She does.

"Count it."

She takes a minute to do so, then says, "Twelve hundred, fifty-five."

"Give it here."

She hands it over.

Then he says, "Let's check the medicine cabinet."

They do, and he takes three of Nancy's prescriptions. Then says, "I'll want a pair of panties."

She leads him back to the dresser, opens a drawer.

"Not *hers*," he says. "*Yours*."

She leads him upstairs to her room, opens her dresser drawer. He selects a pair, stuffs them in his pocket, then glances around her room, but takes nothing. Then they go back downstairs.

"Where's your mom's purse?"

"Kitchen."

"Show me."

Nancy's purse yields $121 in cash. Next, they check the garage, where he finds $28 in the consoles of their cars. Then it's back to the den where he tells Ryan to stand up and has Lindy dig through his pockets for cash, which adds $84 to the take.

The other guy who talks says, "How much all together?"

"A .38 caliber handgun, $1,488 in cash, three prescriptions, and a pair of Lindy's panties."

He removes them from his pocket, dangles them from his fingertips for all to see.

The gunmen ogle them a moment, then the one who talks says, "We should take their cell phones."

"Are you crazy? The minute we turn them on the cops will have our location."

"I thought they weren't gonna tell the cops."

"*I* think they won't, but let's not place too much temptation in their paths."

"What if they call the cops the minute we leave?"

"Good point. We'll put their phones in the mailbox when we go. That'll give us time to get away."

"We should throw them on the roof."

The leader shakes his head. "You think the neighbors might wonder why Ryan's on the roof in the middle of the night? And what if one of the phones starts ringing while it's on the roof? Think that might raise suspicion?"

"We could turn them off."

"Yes we could. But there's no need for the roof. We'll turn them off now and put them in the mailbox when we leave."

"What about their jewelry?"

"Too easy to trace."

"I vote we kill them."

"Tell you what: if they say one word about what happened tonight to anyone at all...you guys can kill them while I punish Lindy. How's that?"

The gunman shrugs.

The leader tells his three victims to stand, then directs them to the master bedroom, forces them into the closet, tells them to sit on the floor. As the gunmen stand over them, weapons aimed a foot from Ryan and Nancy's faces, the man removes their handcuffs and puts them in his backpack. Then he collects their cell phones, turns them off, and says, "I'm going to trust you to stay put for fifteen minutes, and to never speak of this to anyone: not your friends, your relatives, or each other. Forget it ever happened...or you'll wish you had."

"Thank you," Ryan says.

"Thank your daughter. She's the one who saved your asses tonight."

Chapter 3

LIKE A GRADE-SCHOOLER losing a fight to the class bully, Lindy doesn't start crying till the threat is over. By then, she and her parents are deep into a group hug. For several minutes, no words are spoken. Then Lindy crawls to the door, raises her arm, feels around for the light switch. She finds it, turns it on. Then she crawls back to her parents. Dad whispers, "I love you both so much."

Lindy whispers, "I know. Me too."

"Are you okay?" he asks.

"Yes."

"He didn't..."

"No."

"Thank *God!*" Nancy says.

For five minutes the Bissels remain on the floor, saying nothing, grateful to be alive. Then Ryan says, "What do we know about them?"

Lindy says, "There were three men, young, I think, each about six feet tall. The two who talked were white."

Nancy says: "What are you *doing?*"

"Taking inventory," Ryan says.

"What the hell's *that* supposed to mean?"

John Locke

"These men have our personal information. There's no limit to the damage they can do. They can steal our identities. Access our bank accounts. Cash out our insurance policies. Clean out our investment accounts. We need to figure out what we know about them."

"You're not going to the *police?*"

Ryan says nothing.

"Are you *insane?*"

"I don't know what to do. Probably nothing. But as long as we're sitting here it makes sense to review everything we noticed that can help us later on."

"Like what?"

"If these men are local, it would be easy for them to follow us. We have a good read on the speaker's voice. If I ever hear it again, I'll recognize it. Won't you?"

As Nancy starts crying again, Lindy's thinks: *The guy was right. Mom's the weak link.*

"You were with him the longest," Ryan says. "What can you tell us?"

Lindy thinks it through. "He was definitely the leader. He seemed reasonable, and...mostly respectful."

"*Respectful?*" Nancy says. "He took your fucking *underpants!* Why?"

"To intimidate her," Ryan says. "It's a threat. Letting her know what could happen if she talks."

"Then why would you even *consider* telling the police?"

Ryan sighs. "I wouldn't. But if the police happen to catch these guys, our testimony could be crucial."

"I think he took them as a souvenir," Lindy says. "I also think we should report it. How would we feel if they kill some other family?"

"Horrible," Ryan says. "Because they probably will. But they'll *absolutely* kill us if they learn we talked. And by the way, we have zero proof anything *happened.* We don't know who they are, where they're from, or what they look like, other than their shapes and height, which are pretty average. We don't know enough to get them *questioned*, much less arrested."

They go quiet for a full minute. Then Lindy says, "They had two assault rifles."

"And a hand gun, and at least two knives," Ryan says. "What else?"

"We know it was their first home invasion."

He looks at her curiously, so she says, "The head guy was upset the others brought assault rifles."

"So?"

"If this had been their *second* home invasion, they would've known what type of weapons to bring." She pauses. "Wouldn't they? Not to mention all that confusion over what to do with our phones."

Ryan and Nancy look at their daughter.

He says, "Go back to school, Lindy. Get a degree in criminology."

For a split second she nearly laughs. But just as quickly, her face clouds. "I'm sorry about this summer. About not graduating. I screwed up. I was scared to move away. Scared to get a job."

"It's okay," Nancy says. "After this, we don't want you to leave."

Lindy says, "I'm sorry I stuck you with the apartment lease. I feel awful about that."

The doorbell rings.

"Fuck!" Ryan says.

"Don't answer it!" Nancy says.

They remain perfectly still. But then the knocking starts.

Lindy says, "We should check it out."

"What if it's *them*?" Nancy says.

"It's not."

"How do you know?"

"They have your house key."

"*What?*"

"He took it off your key ring when he went through your purse."

"They've got our *house* key?"

"I'll change the locks first thing tomorrow," Ryan says.

The knocking continues. Ryan says, "I'll get the door. You guys hide somewhere else, just in case."

He goes to the kitchen, grabs a chef's knife, then walks to the door and says, "Who's out there?"

Chapter 4

A MAN'S VOICE says, "Denny McCoyn."

"What do you want?"

Ryan plants his foot inches from the door and opens it a crack.

Denny says, "A few minutes ago I saw a man standing in front of your house, like maybe he was casing it or something. I hid behind a tree and watched him put something in your mailbox. After he left, I opened it and found three cell phones. Are they yours?"

Ryan would love to ask Denny if he saw the man's face, or possibly his car, but decides against it. Instead, he asks, "Are you a neighbor?"

"I live two streets over. I was walking my dog."

"Kind of late, don't you think?"

"Normally, yeah, but we just got back from dinner. Anyway, I didn't touch the phones, in case they were stolen. Are they yours?"

"Yes."

He angles his body so he can study Ryan's face. "Is everything all right?"

"Yes, of course."

"Then why would someone put your phones in the mailbox at 11:15 at night?"

"He's just a friend, doing us a favor. He upgraded our phones to iOS 10 tonight, and I guess it took him longer than he thought. I'm sure he assumed we'd still be awake, but we went to bed early. He probably knocked on the door, gave up on us and put our phones in the mailbox."

"Want me to get them for you?"

"No thanks. I'm already up. But seriously, thank you."

"No problem. Sorry to wake you."

Ryan looks at the dog. "Who's this?"

"Petey."

"Cute dog."

"If he weren't, he'd be out on the streets for sure. He's a handful, this one."

Ryan says, "Thanks again for checking on us. It was nice of you to worry."

Denny says, "No problem." Five minutes later he presses a button on his phone. When it's answered, he says, "I just spoke to Ryan."

"And?"

"He's cool."

"How'd he explain the phones?"

"Very well. The guy's smart."

"Smart enough to keep his mouth shut?"

"I think so."

"Good. Where's your car?"

"I'm in it."

"What's that sound?"

"My dog. Well, my dad's dog, actually."

"Are you shitting me?"

"He's my alibi."

After a pause, the voice says, "Can you see the front door?"

"Yeah."

"Keep an eye on them."

"For how long?"

"A half hour. And call us if someone shows up."

"What if someone leaves the house?"

"Follow them."

"All right, but next time it's on one of you guys."

"Fair enough."

"Where are you celebrating?"

"My place. Come when you're done. *After* you ditch the dog."

"Save me some booze."

"You got it."

Chapter 5

AFTER A FITFUL sleep, Lindy wakes up thrashing. In her nightmare, two of the hooded attackers pinned her to the floor. She was naked from the waist up and one of them kept flicking her nipples to make them hard while the leader sharpened his knife.

She takes a few deep breaths to calm her nerves, then sits up and acclimates herself to the hotel room where she spent the night. Of course they all should have spent the night in a hotel, but don't you just know her dad would insist on defending his castle, and mom would refuse to leave his side. Lindy had no choice: the burglars had the house key, and Lindy was their target. She absolutely had to get out of the house.

She gets up, pees, brushes her teeth, fusses with her hair a minute, then puts on some clothes and calls room service. Nothing fancy, just oatmeal and coffee. As she waits for it to arrive, she thinks about last night, and how things would have gone had she spent the night with her parents. First, they would have canceled their credit cards. Then she and her mom would have slept in the master bed while her dad sat by the locked bedroom door all night holding a baseball bat.

By now, he would have called a locksmith. While waiting for him to show up, he would have held a family meeting to discuss the safety measures they'd have to enact to prevent this sort of thing from ever happening again.

Her mom would have withdrawn. She wouldn't want to leave the bedroom all day. Her fears would eventually turn to anger and there'd be plenty of accusations, including: "This never would have happened if you'd bought that house in the gated community I wanted." She'd spend the whole day trying to convince him to sell the house and move away. Ryan would take the day off and do his best to allay her fears.

She's glad she's in a hotel room, away from the madness.

The coffee's fine, but the oatmeal's cold, so she ignores it. After checking in with her parents she calls Ashley Keck, a shut-in, who has a dozen serious issues and only one friend: Lindy. They talk for an hour, and Lindy takes copious notes.

Now, enjoying an early lunch in the hotel restaurant, Lindy has the sudden, overpowering feeling someone's watching her. She scans the room, but sees nothing to worry about. Then, from directly behind her a voice makes her jump: "Hello, Lindy."

As the hair rises on her arms the man says, "May I join you?"

He doesn't wait for a response. Just sits directly in front of her. No gun, no mask. A regular guy, no more than 21. She glances from side to side.

"The others aren't here," he says. "It's just me."

She studies his face a moment, then says, "What do you want?"

He smiles. "What do you think?"

Chapter 6

THE MAN–IAN KELLER–SAYS, "Were you scared?"

"If you're asking me to grade you as a group, I'd give you an 85. You were good, but there were mistakes."

"Like what?"

"You should have taken our phones immediately."

"Why?"

"I could've recorded your voice a dozen times without being detected."

"No way!"

"Believe it."

"Give me one example."

"I'll give you two: first, when I was on the floor, and you were talking to my parents. Second, the entire time we walked through the house."

"Your phone was in your back pocket. I would have seen you."

"You have ear buds?"

He does, and fishes them out of his pocket.

Lindy hooks them up to her phone, presses a couple of buttons, sits back to watch his expression as he hears:

"Where's the cash?"

"He doesn't keep cash here."

"I guarantee you he has something somewhere."

(Pause) "There's a small box in his study."

"Show me."

(Pause)

"Count it."

(Pause) "Twelve hundred, fifty-five."

"Give it here."

(Pause) "Let's check the medicine cabinet."

Keller says, "You were stupid to record that."

She shrugs.

"Why did you?"

"Because I could. And I knew you wouldn't believe me without proof."

He frowns. "What else didn't you like?"

"The panties."

"*What!* That was *your* idea!"

"*You* were perfect. But the twins—"

"What?"

"They didn't sell it."

"What do you mean?"

"You held them up, the twins stared at them, then Rayburn said, 'What about their cell phones?'"

"So?"

"The whole point of the panties is to threaten the daughter, outrage the father, and terrify the mother. The twins should have made a bigger deal about it. They need to act creepy. *Beyond* creepy."

"I thought they did a pretty good job of leering."

"Who can say? They had masks on, remember? All we could see was their eyes. Rayburn should have said something."

"Like what?"

"I don't know, but you're actors. Work it out."

"They had plenty to say afterward."

"Like what?"

"Trust me, you don't want to know. You'd never look at them the same way, ever again."

"Whatever they said, write it down. Maybe it's something we can use."

"Okay, but prepare to be disgusted. Anything else?"

"Yeah. When I unbuttoned my blouse you said 'Relax!'"

"So?"

"I know we had a deal, and I appreciate you sticking to it, but if that happens in real life, don't stop the daughter. It's incongruous."

"What's that mean?"

"Out of character. First you won't let me unbutton my blouse. Minutes later, you're holding up my panties, threatening rape."

"What's the word?"

"Incongruous."

"Incongruous. Fine. What else?"

"You went off script with the personal information. The social security numbers, dates of birth. I don't like it."

"Really? 'Cause I thought it was a nice touch."

"I disagree. You're almost begging them to go to the cops. It's one thing to rob people, quite another to steal their identities."

"You don't think it works as a supplemental threat?"

"No. I—" Lindy frowns. "You did that to threaten *me*, not them."

He smiles. "Well, in this line of work you can't be too careful. It's always nice to have insurance if one of your partners decides to turn state's evidence."

"You'd do that to my parents? Sell their personal information?"

"In a heartbeat, if you burn me. And I'd expect you to retaliate against me if I ever sold *you* out. But let's not make a big deal out of this. If our hearts are true, neither of us has anything to worry about."

"What about the twins?"

"What about them?"

"They scare me."

"I can handle them."

"You're sure?"

"No. But I'm confident."

He reaches into his pocket, removes a wad of cash, peels off $380, slides it across the table. "Your share, from last night."

"By my count it's $372."

He shrugs. "So you'll owe me eight bucks. Big deal."

"What about the gun and pills?"

"In my car. You can get them when we leave."

She nods, then lowers her voice. "Were those *real* assault rifles?"

"They sure as shit were!"

"Why would amateur actors have assault rifles?"

He looks around the room, then whispers, "Think you can say assault rifles a little louder?"

She smiles. "Probably. If I wanted to."

He says, "They're gun nuts. They were showing off, trying to impress us. I told them to bring handguns next time."

Lindy says, "Actually, I like those."

"Really?"

"It's intimidating. I nearly peed myself."

"So you're saying keep the—he whispers—assault rifles?"

"Yes. If you're certain the twins can handle them safely."

"They seem pretty competent."

"Okay then."

"Great! They'll be thrilled. Now what do you have for *me?*"

Lindy smiles, removes a folded sheet of paper from her handbag, gives it to him.

Chapter 7

"TERRI WILCOX?" HE says. "Who's she?"

"One of my former sorority sisters."

Keller scans the address. "Indianapolis?"

Lindy nods.

"Are they wealthy?"

"Her grandfather's wealthy. She's just rich."

"What's the difference?"

"The rich have millions, but the wealthy have so much they have to estimate their net worth."

"I guess that explains why you never hear about get-wealthy schemes. Tell me again why we've avoiding the ones with the most money?"

"Because they typically live in gated communities, have better security, and their address books are filled with the sort of contacts that could do us harm."

"Like who?"

"Senators, Congressmen, law enforcement...possibly even hitmen."

Keller laughs. "Hitmen?"

"According to my dad, every great fortune starts with murder."

"Your parents are rich, right?"

"No. They're comfortable. Again, big difference."

"Where does comfortable rank?"

"Under two million."

"So your contacts are what?"

"Mostly comfortable, and some are rich."

Keller looks around, makes sure no one's listening. "Just to be clear: from now on we can take their jewelry, correct?"

"Yes. And anything else you can convert to cash."

He reads the rest of the page, then smiles. "The mom has a safe in her closet?"

Lindy grins.

"You know this for a fact?"

"I've seen it."

"When?"

"I've spent several weekends there over the past four years."

"Cool. That's what I call a good lead."

"All my leads are good."

"You said you had a dozen of these?"

"No. I said hundreds. With an s. I wasn't just a sorority girl in college, I was president of my sorority, which means we've got an endless supply of victims, as long as you guys don't screw up, get greedy, or hurt someone."

"Got it." He folds the paper back up and puts it in his pocket.

Lindy says, "I've got something else for you."

Chapter 8

LINDY REACHES INTO her purse, pulls out another folded piece of paper, hands it to him.

"What's this?" Keller says.

"Diagram of Terri's house. Open it later."

Keller shakes his head. "You're amazing!"

"Thanks. Okay, so Terri's 22, has a younger brother, Ethan, 16. Mom and Dad are Joe and Kim. He's overweight, possible heart condition, so be careful. If someone dies, we're screwed."

Keller nods.

"The parents usually go out to dinner on the weekends. Terri may or may not be home on any given night, and Ethan's a wild card."

"What do you mean?"

"Like I said, he's 16. He might be spending the night with friends or might have friends staying with him."

"Maybe we should watch the house on a Friday night, wait till Joe and Kim go out, and if no one comes over, we can break in and deal with the kids."

"I don't like it."

"Why not? They'd be a snap."

"I agree. But they'd also tell their parents they were robbed. And their parents will call the cops."

"Why?"

"Because that's how parents are: if it doesn't happen to *them*, it's different. Our plan is predicated on scaring the shit out of the parents. They have to truly believe they're gonna die. When you give them a chance to live, they'll be relieved, but after you leave they'll be outraged. That's why you have to convince them their daughter's at risk." She smiles. "By the way, that was good adlibbing about slicing off my nipples. Gave me nightmares. All my contacts have daughters my age or slightly younger, so keep that in your script."

He nods. Then says, "I worry about them reporting the jewelry. That shit has sentimental value to women."

"That's why you have to be respectful."

"What do you mean?"

"We *talked* about this, Ian."

"Tell me again."

Lindy sighs. "Grab a handful of jewelry and start to put it in your backpack, then act like you feel sorry for the wife. Tell her you're only going to take one piece."

"That's insane! We didn't talk about that!"

"Not in so many words, but I've been thinking about it. Like you say, jewelry has sentimental value. If you only take one, they'll be grateful."

"I think we should take four pieces. One for each of us."

"Of course you do, but now you've got a problem."

"What's that?"

"If you take four expensive pieces of jewelry, Kim and Joe will absolutely file a claim. And they'll eventually confess they were robbed because who loses four pieces of jewelry in the same night? Then the police will get involved, and we'll have to stop."

Keller frowns. "I thought you said we could take their jewelry."

"Yes. One piece. You're gonna tell Joe and Kim if they promise to keep their mouths shut about the robbery, you'll only take one. That way they can report it as lost, instead of stolen. And they will. So make sure the piece you keep is an outstanding one. Something we can unload for at least ten grand."

He nods, reluctantly.

"Trust me," Lindy says. "They'll be thankful they only lost the one piece."

Keller says, "Rayburn and Claiburn won't like it."

"Better to be safe than greedy."

"Do the Wilcoxes have any guns?"

"I don't know. But if so, don't take them."

"Why not?"

"They'll be registered."

"So?"

"Again, Ian: we're robbing them, but we don't want to give them a strong enough reason to report it. If you cripple a man, he'll come after you. If you allow him to keep everything except his cash and a piece of jewelry, and threaten to rape and disfigure his daughter, he'll fall in line."

"Rayburn and Claiburn will say we're leaving too much on the table. Especially the guns."

"Rayburn and Claiburn are short-sighted. Some of these families are bound to have thousands in cash, and possibly gold and silver coins. You can take all those things. My guess is you'll be able to walk out with at least $10,000 to $20,000 worth of coins, cash, and the piece of jewelry at every home I give you. That's $3,000 to $5,000 for each of us, every time. With very little risk."

"Maybe if they saw your entire list."

"Excuse me?"

"If you turn over your list of contacts the twins would feel better about the long-term prospects."

Lindy frowns. "Do I really need to dignify that comment with a response?"

"Yes. Because they already told me to ask you for it."

"If I turn over my list, you'll have no reason to keep me in the deal. I already expect to be cheated, but I won't be left out completely."

"What do you mean you expect to be cheated?"

"*Seriously*, Ian? Surely it's crossed your mind I won't be with you when you rob these homes. So I'll have to take your word for how much you get. But my ace in the hole is this: every time we meet, if I'm not satisfied with my share, I'll stop cooperating. We'll end the partnership, and you guys can go back to being unemployed actors."

For a while, he says nothing. But later, quietly, he says, "I would never cheat you."

She laughs. "Of course you will. Just don't insult me when you do."

He winks. "I keep forgetting how smart you are."

"Smart enough to know acting and bullshit when I see them."

He changes the subject: "How'd it go with your parents? Did it work?"

"You mean did it warm their hearts that I saved their lives during the fake home invasion? Absolutely! Did it get them off my back about flunking out? Yes. Are they still gonna make me move to Dallas? No. So yeah, it worked perfectly."

"Plus you got $400."

"Yes. And you guys got the same, plus a ton of real-life experience."

"When do you want to meet again?"

"After you rob the Wilcoxes."

"When should we do that?"

"You tell me."

"How about Friday night, after Joe and Kim come home from their night out on the town? They'll be tired, maybe a little drunk, one or both of the kids might be gone, or sleeping."

28

Lindy nods. "Sounds good. Let's do all the jobs that way from now on."

He smiles, clearly pleased she approved his idea. "So we'll meet Saturday. What time?"

"Noon. You know the Cinemax Theaters?"

"Yeah."

"Let's meet in the parking lot. I'll circle once, then park. You'll climb in, tell me what happened, and we'll settle up."

"I'll be there," he says, but remains seated.

Lindy says, "Anything else?"

"Yeah. Don't get creeped out, but I was wondering if you'd consider going out with me sometime."

"You mean like a date?"

"Yeah."

"No."

He shrugs.

Chapter 9

Saturday.

Noon.

Parking Lot, Cinemax Theaters.

AFTER DRIVING A slow circle around the parking lot, Lindy pulls into a space between two empty cars and waits. Moments later Keller approaches, showing her a "thumbs-up." She clicks the unlock button. He opens the door and slides into the passenger seat beside her.

"You look pleased," she says.

"Couldn't have gone better!"

"Tell me."

"It was really weird. We rented two cars. Rayburn and I parked one of them where we could keep an eye on the house, and Claiburn followed Joe and Kim on their date."

"Where'd they go?"

"Dinner party."

"What about Terri and Ethan?"

"They were home, but we didn't know that till later. So anyway, Claiburn called us when Joe and Kim were heading home, so we jumped out of the car and hid beside the garage. When the garage door opened we slid in behind their car and waited till they got out. Then Rayburn put his rifle in Kim's face, and I put my .45 in Joe's, and you'll never believe what their first reaction was."

"Tell me."

"They hit the floor, face down."

"Both of them?"

He nods enthusiastically. "We never said a word! They went down at the same time, placed their hands behind their heads, and interlocked their fingers. It was like they'd been through it before!"

"Did they beg you not to hurt them?"

"Nope. Didn't say a word. Just laid there quietly and waited for me to speak."

"Where were the kids?"

"Terri was upstairs, in her room, Ethan was in the basement, playing video games."

"Go on."

"I told Joe and Kim we don't cuff their hands that way, so I cuffed them our way, then took their phones, just like you said, and asked who else was in the house, and they said no one."

"That was stupid."

"No shit! So I told them we were going in and if they were lying we'd make them watch us kill whoever we found."

"Nice. I assume that worked."

"Joe told me the kids were home, and said if I was quiet he'd walk me through the house and let me take whatever I want, and we'd never have to disturb them. But I told him that wasn't going to work. He and Kim would have to stay in the garage and tell me where to find what I wanted. Then, if they promised not to report the break in, I'd spare the kids."

"Obviously he agreed to that."

"Of course. But since we were in the garage, we went through his car, found a gun in the glove compartment, and some cash in the console. We found some cash in Kim and Terri's cars, too."

"What'd you do with the gun?"

"Removed the bullets and put it back."

"I assume you wore gloves."

"Don't insult me, Lindy."

"Sorry. How much cash was Joe carrying?"

"Two hundred."

"Exactly?"

"Yeah. Five twenties, two fifties."

"What about Kim's purse?"

"Sixty-six."

"Did you photograph their driver's licenses?"

"Sure did. Right then and there," he says, proudly.

"Then what happened?"

"We waited a couple of minutes for Claiburn to show. When he tapped on the garage door, I opened it a couple of feet, he slipped in, and I closed it. Then I asked Joe where the kids might be, and he told us. I thanked him for being honest, then told him what I wanted."

"Walk me through it."

"I said, 'Joe, I need to know where you keep the cash, jewelry, gold and silver coins, and any other collections you might have. And don't lie to me, because I'm gonna take my time in there, and if I find something you didn't mention I'm going straight to your daughter's room to show her exactly what I did that got me six years of prison time.' He turned white, and Kim started crying."

"I assume they told you about the safe?"

"She did. And he said that's where they kept everything valuable. I asked for the combination, and he told me the digits: 1622."

"The ages of their kids."

Keller gives her a look. "Now that you mention it..."

"They probably change the combination every year."

"I guess. So anyway, I asked if the alarm was on, and Joe said no, and I asked for the security code in case he was lying, and he said it's the same: 1622. So I entered the house, and he told the truth: no alarm, and I went straight to their bedroom, thanks to your diagram. I found the safe, opened it, and...wow!"

"Let's hear it."

"Five grand in cash, forty gold coins, and a hundred silver dollars."

"And the jewelry?"

"She had a ton, but I did what you said: I grabbed a handful, then pretended to take pity on her, and said if they promised to never speak about the robbery—even to their kids—I'd let them keep all but one piece, and she could file insurance it, and claim she'd lost it. And you were right: she was grateful."

"You picked the piece to keep?"

He pauses, sensing a trap. "Yes."

"Good."

"It's okay?"

She nods. "Good job, Ian. Let's settle up."

He hands her an envelope. "Your share of the cash comes to $1,354.00." He reaches into his pocket, pulls out 25 silver dollars and 10 gold coins, and hands them to her.

"How much are these worth?" she asks.

"Brace yourself: based on yesterday's spot price, the 10 gold coins are worth $13,425!"

"Wow!"

"No shit, wow!"

"And the silver?"

"They're Morgans."

"So?"

"As of yesterday, yours are worth approximately $17,500!"

"Wait: mine alone?"

"Yup. Altogether, the coins I just handed you are worth $30,925.00!"

She grins. "Unbelievable!"

He high-fives her. "Beats the hell out of a 9 to 5, wouldn't you say?"

"It's more than I expected to earn my first full year. How'd it go with Terri's panties?"

"Huh?"

Lindy frowns.

Chapter 10

"AFTER YOU PUT the cash, coins, and jewelry in your backpack, what did you do?"

Keller looks at her blankly. "What do you think?"

"I hope you stayed on script. I hope you brought the parents in the house, sat them on the couch in their den with one of the twins guarding them. Then I hope you went to the basement and put a gun in Ethan's face, took his phone, and forced him upstairs and sat him in the den with his parents. Then I hope you went upstairs, threatened Terri with rape and murder, confiscated her phone, and made her give you a pair of her panties, which you flourished in front of her family, Rayburn, and Claiburn. At which time Rayburn would not only leer, but say something that turned their stomachs. And the reason I hope you did all these things is because without a credible threat of *rape*, this is just an armed robbery." She sighs. "And I can tell by your face you didn't do any of those things."

Keller starts to say something, then changes his mind and says, "No. We didn't. But Joe and Kim were as grateful as your parents were. They swore if we didn't involve the kids they'd never say a word."

She rolls her eyes.

"You had to be there, Lindy, and you weren't. But if you *had* been, you'd have done the exact same thing."

"Not true."

"Dragging the kids into it wasn't necessary."

"I'll tell you what happened, Ian. You hit the jackpot with the cash and coins. You were so excited you couldn't wait to leave. That's why you didn't involve the kids."

He takes a deep breath. "Look: it's easy to sit here the next day in the comfort of your car and criticize the decisions I made in the heat of the moment. But like I said, you weren't there. You didn't see their faces. But I did. And they're not gonna report it. I guarantee it."

Lindy puts her face in her hands. "You're dead wrong, Ian. They're gonna tell the cops. No. Let me rephrase: they've *already* told the cops."

"Well, I guess we'll just have to agree to disagree."

"Don't pout, Ian."

"*What?* Fuck *you*, Lindy!"

Her eyes blaze, and she nearly gets sucked into saying something supremely offensive. But his clenched fists and facial expression remind her she doesn't really know him that well, not to mention the twins. She's suddenly acutely aware of her vulnerability: the angry, unstable man sitting less than three feet away is physically capable of killing her with his bare hands. So she swallows her annoyance and gives herself a moment to calm down. When she finally speaks, her voice is steady, and controlled: "You're right," she says. "I wasn't there. But I was absolutely in my parents' closet last week, and I saw how my dad's attitude changed the minute you guys left. He asked me and Mom to review everything that happened. By the time we left the closet, he knew your height and weight, and the color of your eyes. And it didn't escape Mom's notice that the twins had identical eyes."

"You never thought to mention this before?"

"No, but it's human nature. Every victim wonders if he should report a crime. And anyway, I was there to control the situation. Dad was being a guy: someone broke into his home, threatened his family, stole his possessions. He was right on the edge of going to the police. Any guess what stopped him?"

"You?"

"No. In fact, I told him he *should* report it."

"*What?*"

"I was testing my theory, and it worked: Mom stepped in. And you know what she brought up? The panties. 'He took your fucking *underpants!*' she said, mimicking her mom's voice. 'Why would you even *consider* telling the police?'"

Keller suddenly looks nervous. "What should we do?"

"Cover our tracks."

"How?"

"Do you have the jewelry with you?"

"No."

"What did you take?"

"Diamond bracelet."

"We need to get it into the general population."

"What do you mean?"

"We need to take it back to Indianapolis and place it where it'll get found and fenced."

"Why?"

"If Joe Wilcox contacted the police, they'll put the word out, and the thief will probably be caught."

"Yeah, but the cops will be looking for three men, not one."

"It'll still throw them off our scent. Meanwhile, we'll stay out of Indy. At least till we know it's safe."

She fiddles with her phone a minute. Keller asks, "How many of your contacts are in Indiana?"

"Most of them."

He frowns. "I don't want to ditch the bracelet. I saw a similar one online and it's selling for twenty thousand. We can probably get at least ten for it."

"*Half?* From a *fence?* No way. You'd be lucky to get four grand."

"That's still a lot of cash."

"It's not worth the risk. We need to ditch it."

"The twins won't go for it."

"Fuck the twins."

"I say we wait. There's no reason to assume Joe and Kim told the police. And I still say they didn't."

Lindy says, "I've got worse news."

"What now?"

Chapter 11

"WE NEED TO ditch half the gold and silver coins."

"*What*? Are you *crazy*?"

"No. And let's remember which of us put our group at risk. Here's what I know: the police are going to contact every coin shop and pawn shop in the country. The minute any of us tries to cash in a Krugerrand or Morgan silver dollar the shop owner will contact the police, and it'll be over for us. Unless you trust the twins not to cash in their coins for several years."

"Lindy, look at me: there *is* no situation. The Wilcoxes were scared stupid. I can't express how happy they were that we didn't kill them and didn't involve their kids. We know their names. We know where they live. And when I gave them the line about being in prison for six years, Kim went ballistic. Believe me, *they're* not the problem, Lindy. *You* are!"

"Oh really! How so?"

"You're walking around acting like some sort of Mafia mastermind who knows how much fences pay for jewelry, and everything else for that matter, and you constantly put us down."

"How do I put you down?"

"Are you being serious right now? I told you a thousand times to call me Keller. Everyone calls me Keller. But not you. You call me Ian. And all you ever do is criticize me. You're so full of yourself it's ridiculous! You're smug and cocky and it's not just me: the twins are also sick and tired of all your bullshit. Yeah, you've got the contacts. But that's the *only* thing you bring to the table, because you're weak, pampered, and you have no experience or skills. But we've been catering to you, and somehow you got the impression you're in charge. Well, you're not! We don't *need* you, Lindy. You're quick to brag about your precious contacts, but the truth is you're getting paid awfully goddamn well for selling out your sorority sisters. You're giving us *names*, but *we're* the ones doing the heavy lifting. We're the ones taking all the chances and putting our lives on the line. You think you're tough, barking out orders? You wouldn't last five minutes doing what we do. We'd be in the house, cuffing the parents, and you'd still be on the porch, wetting your pants. You don't like the way we do things? Fine. Walk away. We'll survive just fine without you."

"Nice speech."

"Fuck you! You know what you are? A cunt!"

"How sweet. Makes me wonder why you asked me out last week."

"You really don't know! I wanted to *fuck* you. But I never *liked* you."

"Wow, that's so romantic! If only you'd phrased it that way last week. Maybe I would have said yes."

"You want to be an outlaw, but you're just a privileged brat who's never worked a day in her life."

"I think your argument would be stronger if you and the twins had ever held a job. But last I checked you were all unemployed actors."

"Blow me."

"Nice comeback."

He reaches for the door handle. "I'm out of here, bitch!"

"Fine. Good riddance. But before you go, you'll want to see this."

She hands him her phone. He stares at the screen a minute, then blanches. "Who's Misty?"

"Terri Wilcox's best friend."

"What the fuck am I looking at?"

"Snapchat."

Keller reads the message again:

OMG! My best friend's parents got robbed at gunpoint last night!

His eyes go wide. He coughs so hard he drops her phone. Then yells "*Fuck!*" and punches her dashboard. "*Fuck!*" Punches it again. "*Fuck!*" Punches it a third time. And once more, for good measure, except this time he yells: "*Shit!*"

Then he starts crying.

Crying?

Lindy watches in disbelief, thinking: *This is the guy I was afraid of, moments ago?*

"Calm down," she says.

But he can't. He's beyond help. He's snuffling and sobbing, and leaking snot all over his shirt. So she does what she used to do when her girlfriends got dumped by their boyfriends: she waits till he cries himself out, then begins the long, slow process of restoring his shredded ego. She reassures him it's not over. "Everything's gonna be fine," she says. "I can get us out of this."

"*How?*"

"Nothing has to end, and no one has to get caught. But you *will* have to swallow your pride and allow me to make the decisions. Because despite what you and the twins think about me, I'm *tougher* than you think, *smarter* than you think, and I'm a lot *better* at this than you think. And that's because I understand human nature. You don't get to be two-time president of the top sorority on campus without being a student of people. And let's not forget: I *know* these families. So yeah, I have a pretty good idea how they're gonna act when you put a gun to their heads."

If Lindy had less confidence, Keller would hate her even more. But while she's the Queen of Cunts, she's also smarter than anyone he's ever met. Not to mention she's hotter than a West Texas bonfire, and he'd give his left nut to fuck her. And amazingly, she seems not the least bit concerned over this devastating development. In fact, she *called* it, based on nothing more than his explanation of the robbery. Much as he hates to admit it, there's something in her attitude that inspires trust. He *does* believe she'll make the right decisions. So, just as she advised, he swallows his pride, snuffles one last time, then says, "If you can fix this, you can run things from now on."

"What about the twins?"

"If they refuse, we'll find someone else."

"Thanks, Ian. Let's give them a call and see where they stand."

Chapter 12

FORTY-FIVE MINUTES LATER they're walking the Nature Trail at Sawyer Park. To outside eyes they look like four friends hanging out. Lindy tells them Joe Wilcox almost certainly reported the robbery, but if not, he soon will, since his daughter's best friend blasted it over the Internet.

Rayburn says, "He wasn't supposed to tell his daughter."

Keller says, "I would have bet against it."

Lindy says, "It's that whole mother-daughter dynamic."

"What do you mean?"

"Kim probably told her."

Rayburn says, "On Snapchat that Misty girl said it happened to her best friend. She didn't name Terri Wilcox."

"No, but she said enough. It's definitely gonna come out if it hasn't already."

Keller says, "Lindy wants us to go back to Indianapolis and ditch the bracelet. Whoever tried to fence it will get arrested."

Lindy says, "It might not stick, but it'll keep the cops distracted for a while, chasing down that guy's circle of contacts."

"I like it," Rayburn says.

"You won't like the next part," Keller says. He looks at Lindy. "Tell them."

"The gold and silver coins," she says. "My first choice would be to scatter half of them all around Indianapolis. That'll really screw up the cops' investigation."

"That's not gonna fly," Rayburn says. "What's your second choice?"

"We'd make a deal among ourselves not to cash them in for at least three years. And when we do, it can't be more than one silver dollar at a time, and never in the same city. And no more than three Krugerrands at a time, and never at the same place where we cashed a Morgan."

"You're totally overreacting. We can't possibly be the only people in the country trying to sell Morgans and Krugerrands."

"No. But I'd rather all the other sellers get questioned for years before we start."

"What if we need the money?" Claiburn says, and since he virtually never speaks, they all take a moment to turn and acknowledge him.

Lindy says, "We didn't have *any* gold or silver twenty-four hours ago. We should pretend we still don't have any. Think of it as a nest egg. In the meantime, we'll rob some more families, get some more cash. Deal?"

"I'm in," Keller says.

"How about you guys?"

The twins look at each other. Rayburn says, "We'll want to think about it and let you know. What's the other thing you wanted to talk about?"

"Terri."

"What about her?"

"She told her friend about the robbery."

"So?"

"She needs to be punished."

"How?"

"She deserves to be killed."

"I'm not killing anyone!" Keller says.

"Would you beat the shit out of her?"

"Maybe."

"Twins?"

Rayburn says, "Sure. If it includes fucking her."

Lindy's face registers disgust. "Out of the question."

"Why?"

"The cops would be able to match your DNA, and you'd immediately be tied to the rape *and* the home invasion."

"They don't have our DNA on file," he says.

"Not yet. But if you're ever arrested for anything you'll be fingerprinted, swabbed, and eventually linked to these crimes."

"Okay," he says. "No sex."

"So you'll beat her up. Severely, if there's time."

"Who gets to hit her first?" Rayburn says.

"Draw straws."

"What if we get caught?" Claiburn says.

"You're a chatty little thing, once you get started."

His face reddens.

"My advice? Wear ski masks. Gloves. Long-sleeve shirts."

Keller says, "How are we going to isolate her?"

"You're gonna follow Misty. She and Terri are always together. Follow her for a day or two and she'll eventually lead you somewhere you can beat the shit out of both of them."

"*Both* of them?"

"Misty shouldn't have posted the news."

Rayburn says: "While we're doing all the grunt work, what'll *you* be doing?"

"Creating profiles of the next six families we're going to rob. Complete with maps of their homes and neighborhoods."

"You have all that information in your head?"

"Most of it. Google Maps and social media will supply the rest." She stops walking, forcing them to stop and look at her. "I know you think I'm just lying around all day waiting for you to bring me money, but I'm doing a lot more than providing names and addresses. You're getting specialized knowledge: details about the parents and siblings and their schedules. Layouts of the homes. And don't you find it useful to know if your victims have a safe?"

"Whatever."

The three men leave together, and Lindy continues walking the trail. When she gets back to her car, Keller calls her and says:

Chapter 13

"WE'RE NOT GOING to do it."

"Do what?"

"Beat up the girls."

"Why not?"

"We're not in the *Mafia*, Lindy."

"I see."

"Don't pout, Lindy," he says, triumphantly. Throwing her words back at her.

Instead of taking the bait she says, "You're right. I've been giving you far too much credit. Maybe you should tell me what you are so I'll know exactly what I'm dealing with."

"We're twenty-year-old college dropouts, not gangsters. We don't need to *punish* young women, or send a message, or whatever the fuck you're calling it. We threatened Joe and Kim, they called our bluff, and...it's over. What's done is done. We got our money. As long as we stay away from them, we'll almost certainly get away with it."

"I see. So where are you right now?"

"Driving home."

"What about the bracelet?"

"We've got a problem with that, too. It's too risky. Someone might see us."

Lindy shakes her head in disgust, even though there's no one there to see it. "Let me ask you this: do you and the twins agree it makes sense to plant the bracelet somewhere?"

"Yes."

"Then give it to me. I'll drive there and do it myself."

"When?"

"Right now."

Keller hesitates. "No offense, but how do we know you won't keep it for yourself?"

"Ride there with me and watch me do it. Then you can help me with something else."

"What?"

"I need you to stand guard outside a women's restroom."

"Why?"

"So I can beat the shit out of Terri Wilcox without being interrupted."

Keller's silence makes her smile. Clearly, she's thrown him for a loop. Lindy waits for him to recalibrate his opinion of her, and when he does, he says: "I thought we just agreed not to beat her up."

"*You* guys agreed. Not me."

"You could be putting us all in danger."

"I'll be discreet. I'll put a ski mask on before following her into the restroom."

"Which restroom are we talking about?"

"I don't know yet. But you know us girls. We like to primp. And fluff. And sometimes we actually pee."

"No."

"Excuse me?"

"I'm not going to help you."

Lindy grits her teeth. "Fine. I'll do it myself."

Keller pauses again. Then says, "Why's this so *important* to you? We gain *nothing* by beating her up. It's all risk, no reward."

"I disagree."

He pauses. "You could do it?"

"What?"

"Assault your friend?"

"Of course."

"Severely?"

"It's just business, Ian."

"Keller," he says. "I'm *Keller*, goddamnit!"

Lindy says nothing.

Keller says, "How many times am I gonna have to tell you that?"

"It won't matter. I'll never call you Keller. Want to know why? Because Ian's a pussy name, and Keller's for tough guys. So get used to it, *Ian*. Until you grow a pair, that's your name, far as I'm concerned."

"Maybe I already have. I said no to *you*, just now."

"Yes you did. But 90 minutes ago you were in my car, crying like a little bitch. You agreed to let me run things and said if the twins refused to accept it, we'd find someone else."

"I changed my mind."

"Clearly."

"We've opted for a democracy." Smugly, he adds: "By the way, we decided to fence the bracelet."

"Oh, really?"

"That's right. We voted."

"I see. Well, if you *do*, split it three ways."

"Why?"

"Because if you fence the bracelet, I'm out."

"What are you *talking* about? You can't just walk away."

"Are you gonna fence the bracelet?"

"Yes."

"Then these are the last words you'll ever hear me say."

He waits to hear her last words, but all he's getting is empty air. Which tells him those *were* her last words.

He calls her back.

No answer.

He yells "*Fuck!*" and nearly punches his steering wheel, but stops himself just in time. He looks around for something softer, and settles on the passenger seat, but can't reach it without unbuckling his seat belt, and can't do that unless he pulls over and parks the car. So he does, and makes a fist, but by then, the mood's been killed. In the end, he settles for yelling "*Fuck!*" two more times, and nothing gets punched.

Chapter 14

AS LINDY STEERS her car onto I-65 North, heading to Indianapolis, the reality of her bluster sets in. Ian was right about one thing: she *is* a wannabe. A poser. At least she always *has* been, till now. But if she can muster the courage to rough this girl up, and do so without being seen or identified, she will have taken a major step forward in her new career.

It won't be easy.

The thought of approaching Terri—or anyone—in a physical confrontation makes her stomach clench. It's terrifying, and completely out of character: she's never been in a fight, never been slapped, never even had her hair pulled in anger.

Flying blind, she'll have to rely on three elements: surprise, superior force, and her acting skills. The surprise will be easy: Terri's not expecting to be ambushed in a public restroom. Superior force will be her dad's unloaded gun she packed in her duffel along with three days' worth of clothes, and her acting skills were honed between the sheets long before she took summer classes with Ian and the twins.

Lindy can't emphasize the acting skills enough. She saw first-hand how well it worked for Ian, who, after just weeks of practice, developed a thoroughly convincing tough guy voice and swagger that makes him appear ten years older than he is, while employing a perfect blend of authority and menace.

In fact, he frightened her today, even though she *knows* he's a phony.

Her dad's gun is neither big nor heavy, which is good, since she has no clue how to load it, much less shoot it. But what she *does* know about guns—courtesy of Ian in her own home last week—is they don't have to be loaded. You pull a gun on someone, they do what you tell them. Period.

Lindy's phone rings for the fourth time in twenty minutes: It's Ian again. She lets it go to voice mail, and this time he leaves a message. She plays it and laughs. He wants to meet. He'll go with her to Indy. They won't fence the bracelet. They'll do whatever she says.

She ignores him and concentrates on the task at hand: Lindy figures to follow Terri into a restroom somewhere: coffee shop, restaurant, night spot, whatever. Then she'll smack the back of Terri's head with her gun. When Terri goes down, Lindy will kick whatever part of her is unprotected.

And she'll keep kicking her.

Then she'll use a tough-girl voice to appear older, menacing, and dangerous. Before leaving Terri crumpled and bleeding on the floor she'll whisper: "We're watching you, Terri."

That's one way she sees it going down. But another is she follows Terri into the restroom and there are other women in there, so she has to turn around and leave. And maybe she doesn't get another opportunity, and winds up going home, unfulfilled.

Another possibility is Terri spins around at the last moment, recognizes her, and Lindy will have to buy her drinks all night and explain why she's wearing a wig, gloves, and white powder makeup.

A fourth scenario has Terri spinning around, not recognizing Lindy, but pushing her against the wall and beating the shit out of *her*. That *could* happen, since Terri's bigger, stronger, and more athletic. If that happens, hopefully the wig won't come loose, and with any luck

Terri will rush out of the room without taking Lindy's gun, turning it over to the police, or alerting the management.

The final possibility is she'll smack Terri's head with the gun, but because she's inexperienced and scared and so pumped up with adrenalin she'll hit her too hard and Terri will die or suffer permanent brain damage. Then, before Lindy can run out of the restroom, an off-duty transgender policeman chooses that precise moment to enter the ladies room to take a transgender piss. He'll walk in on them, and...

She hasn't bought the wig yet.

She pulls off the Interstate, cuts over to Bloomington, finds a thrift store, and gets what she needs to complete the "look." Bloomington, because it's a college town, and school's just started, and she's less likely to be identified later if something bad happens and the cops start calling thrift stores to see if anyone matching Lindy's description recently purchased a black wig. She's counting on the fact that thrift store clerks see a hundred coeds each week and after years of waiting on them, the faces start blending together, and they all look the same.

Chapter 15

TWO HOURS LATER Lindy checks into one of several hotels located within two miles of Terri's house. She calls her parents to let her know she's spending a couple of nights with a friend, then showers, fiddles with her new wardrobe and makeup till she can barely recognize herself. Then she calls Uber and gets a ride to the airport, rents a car, drives to Terri's neighborhood, parks a block away from Terri's house, and waits.

Lindy knows the make, model, and license plate of Terri's car, courtesy of Ian's phone camera. It's early evening, and with any luck, Terri will want to go out. Of course, it's also possible, even *likely*, that Joe and Kim will keep their kids on a tight leash for a week or two. After all, it was just last night they were robbed. But Terri's 22, single, and won't want to be cooped up with her parents. And, due to Ian's screw up, she wasn't grabbed, thrown to the floor, and didn't have a gun in her face. She wasn't threatened, never saw the attackers, never even knew they'd been in her home. And that makes a huge difference in Terri's perception of the possible danger lurking a block away.

After an hour, she notices two women—neighborhood walkers—approaching her car. She eases out of her parking space and drives back to the rental car dealership to trade cars. "Too small," she tells them. "Let's try a mid-size. And a different color."

Then she drives back to Terri's neighborhood, claims the exact same parking space, sits there twenty minutes, drives two blocks, turns, parks, and remains in her car for another twenty minutes. Back and forth two more times at twenty minutes each, then she finally calls it a night, drives back to the hotel.

It wasn't a complete bust.

The entire time she was on Terri's street she never saw a police car, or one she thought could be unmarked. So the neighborhood walkers never reported her as being suspicious, and the police don't know about the home invasion.

Unless they were monitoring her some other way.

Lindy laughs at herself. Paranoid, anyone?

This criminal world she's entered is so different than the one she inhabited just months ago in college. In some respects, it's like being in high school: she's still living with Mom and Dad, and life is comfortable. If she wanted to, she could sleep in, watch movies and TV, lay out in the sun, swim in the pool, listen to music, attend afternoon acting classes three times a week. Her biggest stress could be figuring out what to eat for lunch.

But there's no money, and Lindy's not wired for laziness. Nor is she wired for working in corporate America, like her friends who are already stuck in part-time, entry-level jobs. To Lindy, it doesn't take a genius IQ to realize minimum wage plus no benefits equals zero opportunity for advancement.

So she started asking around: "Where's the big money?"

One girlfriend said with her killer face and body she could make two thousand bucks a night as a hooker. Two women in her acting class claimed to earn $600 a week as dancers.

"Dancers?"

"Well, okay, technically we're strippers," they admitted, after a round of drinks. But they're bringing home $600 a week for eight hours of actual work. "If you count dancing and flirting as actual work."

After further questioning, Lindy decided it was indeed work, and bad work at that: the place smells, the hours suck, the bouncers and servers get half their tips, the clients are freaky degenerates. The dancers are prime targets for stalkers and rapists, and not only that, but: "We have to blow the boss twice a week."

So, no thanks.

Then one day in acting class she and Ian participated in a skit where they played a husband and wife being robbed in a home invasion. Afterward, during the critique, she listed a number of mistakes the two "gunmen," had made.

The acting coach was impressed.

So was Ian.

So were the gunmen (Rayburn and Claiburn).

They got together after class for drinks and talked about how easy it would be to gain entry and scare the piss out of people in their homes, provided you had detailed knowledge of the people, their habits, and their homes. She told them she had hundreds of college contacts she could research, and dozens she already had intimate knowledge about that she could exploit immediately, if she ever decided to start a life of crime.

The more they talked, the more they liked the idea.

But none of them had criminal backgrounds, so Lindy came up with the idea of a dry run. She volunteered her own parents. They'd been treating her like shit lately, complaining about her lack of ambition, and the money she's cost them, and the time she's wasted... so why not stick it to them and gain some valuable armed robbery experience at the same time?

It was a perfect plan and they executed it with near-precision.

And here they were, practically rock-star home invaders, and they've already fucked it up. Lindy didn't "somehow get the impression" she was the leader, as Ian claimed. In her view, she'd been the leader from day one. *She* took them out for drinks. *She* had the contacts. *She* told them what to do and how to do it, and it worked.

It's not over.

Ian and the twins have finally learned they can't do this without her. Not that she needs further proof, but over the next two hours both Rayburn *and* Claiburn call and leave voice messages.

They're contrite.

Should she call them all back and accept her victory?

No. Better to let them sweat. They've earned this punishment. They're sitting on $32,000 *each* because of her contacts and planning. They've tasted the risk-reward. So no, she's not gonna call them back or answer their calls. Eventually, they'll find her. And when they do, she'll play it cool. She'll say she's putting together a new crew. She'll tell them she's moving on, and she'll wish them well. Maybe they'll leave, maybe they'll talk her into staying.

Or maybe she *will* get a new crew. Actors literally *are* a dime a dozen.

In the meantime, she needs to focus on finding and punishing Terri Wilcox. But she won't be punishing Terri for blabbing about her parents being robbed. Truth is, Terri probably doesn't even *know* her parents were robbed. For more than two hours this evening, there were no cop cars watching the house, or patrolling the neighborhood.

But Terri *does* need to be punished. That was half the reason for robbing her parents. Terri, the perfect girl. Joe's little angel. The one who—on at least one memorable occasion—sucked a guy off in the teacher's parking lot in front of a half-dozen witnesses. Set for life by virtue of being born. The bitch is long overdue for a come-uppance.

Yes, Terri has a best friend named Misty, but no one named Misty sent a Snapchat about her best friend's parents being robbed at gunpoint. Lindy faked the message for Ian's benefit. Had she not done so, Ian would have had the satisfaction of knowing he and the twins did a fine job of containing the victims without her help. She would have lost control of the group and been forced to play the most subservient role in the group.

The plan had been to scare the shit out of Terri. Throw her to the floor. Threaten her. Make her beg for mercy. Lindy wanted more than cash from the Wilcox home invasion: she also wanted the compensation of putting fear in Terri's preppy little heart. Having to live with the constant fear that three scary men are watching your every move, waiting for you to be alone, would be emotionally crippling.

So yes, she and her crew got a nice haul from Terri's parents, but Terri came out of it completely unscathed.

And that's unacceptable.

Lindy falls asleep shortly after midnight, wakes up early, showers, puts on her wig, applies her makeup, and runs a computer search for coffee shops within a two-mile radius of Terri's house.

Chapter 16

PEOPLE ARE CREATURES of habit, and habits die hard. If it were any day of the week but Sunday, Lindy would know where to find Terri between the hours of 8:30 and 10:00 a.m. She'd be in a coffee shop, tapping away on her computer. At least, that was her routine every morning in college. Back then it was homework and answering emails. Now she's probably searching for investments, or a multi-million-dollar company to purchase. But whether it's the atmosphere, the people, or the actual coffee, Terri's addicted to coffee shop mornings.

Except on Sundays.

That was her day to sleep in.

If Terri's still on her college schedule she'll remain in bed till noon, so there's no point surveilling her house. But for those entering the work force as Owner/CEO's, Sunday morning's a great time to scan the business opportunity ads. If Terri's doing that, she'll be doing it in a coffee shop. And since all coffee shops are astonishingly similar, there's no reason to travel a great distance to support one. Which means Terri will be in one of the three closest to her home.

At precisely 8:30 a.m. Lindy gets in her rental car and drives to the first coffee shop on her list and waits in the parking lot for twenty minutes before giving up. Then she drives to the second shop, enters, and looks around the store. And though the place is almost totally devoid of customers, the chick directly across from her in the booth by the widow...is Terri Wilcox.

Lindy whirls around, rushes out the door, and circles the back of the building. She enters the door on the opposite side, the one that passes directly in front of the restrooms. She slips into the one marked Women, enters the first of two stalls, locks the door, sits on the toilet without lowering her jeans, and waits.

What are the chances Terri will enter the restroom before leaving the coffee shop?

Virtually 100%.

What are the chances she'll enter when no other women are in the restroom?

Lindy has no clue.

Nor does she have any idea how long she and Terri might be in the restroom together before someone else enters.

She's shaking.

This is a huge step for her future. Screw it up and she'll end up in jail, and possibly prison. She walks herself through it: step number one: make sure the disguise is working. The wig has to completely cover her hair; the makeup has to change her look without giving the impression she's painted herself a clown face.

She rummages through her purse, locates her lipstick mirror, checks her reflection. But the mirror's too small to give her total confidence, so she takes a huge chance and opens the stall door, rushes to the mirror to make sure she's believable as a pale gothic girl with false eyelashes and dark eyeliner. Then she rushes back to the stall, locks the door, reclaims her seat on the toilet.

Step number two: try to get a view of the door.

She leans forward and puts her right eye next to the narrow gap between the door and the door frame, but the angle's all wrong. No way she'll be able to see Terri until the last possible second. Can she look under the door? No. Not without getting on her hands and knees, which would make her a visible curiosity to anyone who enters the restroom.

She props her lipstick mirror against the bottom edge of the stall and adjusts it until she gets a clear view of the door. If Terri enters, Lindy will be able to identify her.

With that out of the way, she reaches into her purse and removes her gun and practices holding it different ways, trying to determine how to inflict maximum damage without killing Terri or losing her grip. Because if the gun falls to the floor and Terri gets to it first, she could prevent Lindy from getting it back. Lindy would have to run to her car and drive away, and Terri would turn the gun over to the police. The police would trace it to Lindy's dad, and that would seal the deal.

Lindy finally decides to hold it the normal way, and use the butt of the gun to strike the back of Terri's head. As Terri's legs crumple, Lindy will slam the gun into Terri's stomach, kick her in the ribs a couple times, and rake the barrel across her face to bloody her up.

She tries to picture the assault in her mind and realizes it all comes down to the first strike: hit her too hard, she's dead. Hit her too soft, Terri screams. If she screams people come running, the manager detains Lindy, the police arrest her, game over.

Lindy has no idea how much force to use, but decides harder is better.

There's the matter of blood evidence.

Terri's certain to bleed from the initial strike, but will she bleed enough to create blood spatter onto Lindy's arm or clothing?

Doubtful. Unless Lindy hits her too hard, in which case all bets are off.

Suddenly the bathroom door opens...

Chapter 17

IT'S NOT TERRI. It's an older lady, mid-30's who walks past Lindy's stall and enters the one beside her. Lindy's senses are heightened. She's acutely aware of the lady's presence. Hears her breathing. Hears her fiddling with her clothes. Hears her lower her pants. Lindy listens for proof the lady's relieving herself, but nothing happens.

Like Lindy, she's just sitting there quietly.

Lindy waits.

The lady waits.

And then it hits her: the lady's waiting for Lindy to leave so she can have some privacy. So she can have a *bowel movement*. In private.

A *bowel* movement? In a public toilet in a coffee shop on a Sunday *morning*? Who *does* that?

The smart, hygienic thing to do is leave. But Lindy can't leave. She's committed to doing this thing, even if it lands her in prison.

But the lady beside her is no less committed. She won't start shitting till Lindy leaves.

A full minute passes.

Then another.

Then another, and three more. Less than four feet apart, the women sit quietly, like opposing armies engaged in an uneasy cease-fire, each daring the other to make a move.

Lindy figures to have the advantage: she doesn't need to evacuate her bowels. But such is the lady's resolve, her very silence exudes an unnerving confidence, giving the impression she's perfectly willing to engage in a standoff of epic proportions if that's what it takes to win this war of attrition.

Lindy thinks back to her human anatomy class and wonders how long the woman is prepared to suffer for her modesty. At the anus, Lindy recalls, there are two sphincters that control the exit of feces from the colon. The internal sphincter is involuntary, while the external is voluntary...to a point.

Lindy intends to force the lady all the way to that point, and beyond.

But the lady's having none of it.

Another minute passes before the lady finally speaks: "I can sit here all day," she says.

"No you can't," Lindy says. Then wonders why she bothered saying anything at all.

"What's your *problem?*" the lady says.

Lindy says nothing.

"You get your jollies listening to people use the bathroom?"

Lindy rolls her eyes.

Another minute passes and the lady says, "I asked you a question, bitch!"

"Fuck you!" Lindy says.

The lady jumps to her feet, pulls her pants up, pushes her stall door open, grabs Lindy's door, and tries to force it open.

"Open the door, you fucking cunt!" she snarls.

When Lindy says nothing the lady kicks it. "I *will* fuck you up!" she says.

The lady assumes Lindy's trapped in the stall, helpless, so she drops to the floor and starts sliding under the stall. She's so preoccupied with gaining entrance she hasn't caught sight of Lindy's gun.

"Now what are you gonna do?" she says, attempting to scramble to her feet.

Lindy slams the butt of the gun against the side of the lady's skull. She falls to the floor and cries out in pain, but not as loudly as Lindy expected. While she has no real desire to hurt her further, the sudden opportunity to practice her ass-kicking technique proves irresistible, so Lindy puts her gun back in her purse and kicks the lady in the stomach as hard as she can, given the limited space.

And the woman defecates.

Thank goodness bathroom stalls open outward, or Lindy would have remained trapped until she could have dragged the lady out of the way. She unlocks the door, steps over the lady, grabs her lipstick mirror, and walks briskly out of the coffee shop. Now, in her car, she looks up, sees no one following her, or taking pictures, or writing down her license plate.

She breathes a sigh of relief, and takes a moment to stare at Terri Wilcox, sitting by the window, typing away on her computer, oblivious to the events around her.

Lindy sighs. Wasn't meant to be. She points her car toward the rental car agency thinking how lucky Terri is: not only was she born rich, she also has two million bucks in a trust fund, courtesy of her grandfather, who owns the international rights to a food additive that enhances the taste and visual appeal of half the canned goods sold in America. Not only that, but she's the apple of her daddy's eye, and has survived not one, but two of Lindy's planned attacks. She can practically hear Terri laughing, giving her the middle finger.

It's a disappointment, but a minor one, because Lindy has other ways to hurt her. Still, she grimaces over the lost opportunity.

Then it hits her: she just committed an assault with a deadly weapon and brutalized a woman in a public restroom. Made her shit herself. Left her lying on the floor, bleeding.

She replays the horrifying scene in her mind, and smiles broadly.

Maybe she *does* have what it takes to head up a gang!

Chapter 18

NOW, BACK IN Louisville, four days have passed with no word from Ian and the twins. Lindy's not devastated over it, just surprised, since they'd been calling nonstop throughout the weekend. But hey, if they're ready to move on, so is she.

Lindy looks up from her blue notebook, takes another sip of her morning latte, and glances at the restroom door. She wonders if anyone's inside.

Lindy's not a violent person, but she has to admit enjoying the heightened sense of confidence her recent experience has given her. With the gun in her purse she now has the confidence to walk into any ladies room in the country and bring someone to her knees.

Lindy's not a mean person, but she's harboring thoughts that are so unlike her. Specifically, she can't stop wondering what it would feel like to follow a complete stranger into a restroom for the purpose of making her do something demeaning. While the lady's doing her business on the toilet, Lindy would wait patiently at the sink. When the lady flushes the toilet, Lindy would remove her gun from her purse and aim it at the stall in a shooter's stance. When the lady opens the stall door she'd be staring down the barrel of Lindy's gun.

Lindy would cock the hammer and motion the lady to her knees. The lady would drop to her knees, and...

Then what?

That's the real question.

Lindy would rob her, of course, but not right away. Because this thing she's feeling is more about power, and the ability to control another person's actions. The lady will fear for her life, having no idea how incredibly benevolent Lindy is.

But it's important the stranger in the bathroom *believes* Lindy would snuff her life and forever alter her world. Lindy tries to comprehend the enormous pain her spontaneous, senseless action would cause. Twenty years from now the lady's husband and children will be different people because of Lindy's actions today. She would, in a very real sense, have altered history, and how many of us can say we've done that?

Of course, that's only if she killed the lady. And for that she'd need bullets.

But the lady won't know Lindy's gun is empty. She'll be terrified. She'll believe she could die at any moment, and will do whatever Lindy says.

Lindy will certainly require some groveling. Otherwise, how can she display her benevolence? In addition, she'll force the lady to perform some type of humiliating act, because if you've got a total stranger on her knees it would be a complete waste not to press that advantage.

She looks around the coffee shop and focuses on a young lady in her mid-twenties, sitting at a table by the fireplace, chattering away on her phone. Lindy pictures the lady ending the call, going to the bathroom, using the toilet. When she exits the stall, she'll gasp, seeing Lindy holding the gun on her. Lindy will motion her to her knees, and the lady will beg her not to hurt her. Lindy will say: "Toss me your purse." The lady will do it. "Roll onto your back." The lady will do it. "Touch yourself." The lady will do it. Lindy will laugh, then empty the lady's wallet, steal her driver's license, and say, "Stay on your back and keep touching yourself for two minutes. If I come back and you're not doing that, I'll kill you. Swear to God!"

The lady will lie there, on the bathroom floor, on her back, touching herself, for at least a minute.

Maybe Lindy will come back after fifteen seconds to check on her. And if the lady isn't doing what she's supposed to do...then what? What will Lindy be forced to do?

Punish her.

She'll pistol-whip her, kick her, and rake her gun barrel across her face like she wanted to do to Terri.

Heady stuff.

She turns her attention back to her notebook. Though she hasn't put any effort into recruiting a new team of actors, she *has* invested her time wisely, mining vast quantities of data from the social media pages of university coeds. The next victim? The Reinholds. As Lindy reviews her notes on Jenny Reinhold, a large shadow crosses her table.

She looks up...

Chapter 19

"DON'T SAY ANYTHING!" Ian says. "Just give us two minutes."

He and the twins take her silence as permission to sit. As they do, Lindy focuses on Claiburn's smiling face.

Something's up.

Ian says, "We had a long talk and quickly came to the conclusion we can't do this without you." He studies her facial reaction, which yields nothing, so he says, "You're the one who brought us together, the one who made it all happen. You're the one with the contacts, and—much as we hate to admit it—you're the one with the brains, as well. Everything you ever said or predicted turned out to be true. What I'm saying...we trust you. Completely."

She looks at Rayburn. He says, "Totally."

Claiburn adds, "One hundred percent."

The young lady at the table by the fireplace gets to her feet. Lindy's eyes track her as she walks to the restroom. She sees her enter, watches the door close behind her. Lindy thinking: *if only I had my wig and makeup. Or a ski mask.*

Ian notices the blue notebook, which she's titled *Every Last Dime*, and grins. "Are those the future victims?"

Lindy says nothing.

Ian says, "How about it?"

"How about what?"

"Can we come back? We'll do whatever you say."

Lindy wonders if he really means it. For example, would he and the twins take turns dropping to their knees and blow each other?

She doubts it.

But she *does* need a crew.

Nevertheless, she says, "Thanks, but I don't think we're a match. I'm putting a new crew together."

"Please?" Rayburn says.

"Sorry."

He looks at Claiburn, who looks at Ian and says, "Tell her."

Lindy rolls her eyes. "Tell me what?"

Ian grins. "We did it."

"Did what?"

He looks at Rayburn, who says, "We beat the shit out of Terri Wilcox. Just like you asked us to."

"*What?*"

"We fucked her up good."

"I don't believe you."

"It's true! I swear!"

"Bullshit."

Ian says, "Show her the pictures."

Lindy says, "You have *pictures?*"

Rayburn takes out his phone, presses a couple of buttons, swipes the screen several times, adjusts the brightness, then hands it to her.

First picture shows Terri's car in a gravel parking lot after dark.

"Where is this?" Lindy says.

"A bar in Indy called *Dovetails*. She's dating one of the bartenders. They kissed outside the bar, then he went back in and we jumped her."

"Did anyone see you?"

"Nope. It's not very crowded on Monday nights."

She swipes the screen to the second photo, which shows Terri on the ground, fetal position, gash on her head, face bloodied.

Lindy can't believe it. She looks up to find them grinning like monkeys flinging shit at their zookeeper. "You did this?"

"Uh huh," Claiburn says. "Swipe again!"

She does, and nearly drops the phone. Her eyes bug out. "Whaaat?"

The photo shows Terri naked from the waist down, her pants and panties around her ankles. She's covering her crotch with her hands.

Ian says, "We knew whatever the deal was between you and Terri, it had to be personal, or you wouldn't have been so upset. So as a gift to you, we decided to humiliate her. Like you said, we couldn't *fuck* her, but..."

Lindy swipes the screen and sees Terri still naked, but face down, and something's— "What's in her ass?"

"Pepper spray!" Ian says.

"*What?*"

"She tried to spray us, but we grabbed the canister from her and shoved it up her ass."

Lindy laughs. "Oh my God! How *big* was it?"

Rayburn says, "Four inches, give or take. But here's a better question: how *wide* was it?"

He laughs.

"Did she scream?"

"She tried, but we wouldn't let her."

"Did she beg you to stop?"

"Many times."

"Did she cry?"

"Like a fuckin' baby!"

Lindy jumps to her feet. "Omigod! I'm so *proud* of you! Come here: group hug!"

After the hug they reclaim their seats and she looks at Ian and says, "Nice job, Keller."

He beams.

She looks at the twins. "Nice job, Ray. Nice job, Clay." She notes their expression. "What's wrong?"

Claiburn says, "*Everyone* calls us Ray and Clay."

"Isn't that what you want?"

"Not from you."

"Well, you've both earned nicknames. What shall I call you?"

They look at each other. Rayburn says, "Same as always."

Lindy cocks her head. "Rayburn and Claiburn?"

They nod.

"I thought you hated those names."

"Only our mom called us that," Claiburn says. "But she died last year, so..."

"You miss hearing it?"

"Yeah."

Lindy smiles. "I'd be honored...so long as you don't call me Mom!" She reaches her hands out. When each twin takes one, she squeezes their hands lovingly.

Keller says, "We also ditched the bracelet."

"Really?"

He nods.

"Thank you."

"You toughened us up, Lindy. You were right, we needed it. Now, the sky's the limit."

Lindy's over the moon. They're finally bonding. Twenty feet behind Keller the bathroom

door opens, and the young lady who'd been sitting at the table by the fireplace is finally leaving. Must have needed some privacy. Much as Lindy would have loved to practice her bathroom assault skills, she realizes there'll be other days, other women, other bathrooms. Plus, if people truly *are* creatures of habit, she knows where to find this particular girl on any given Thursday morning, should the urge arise.

"Who's next?" Keller asks.

Chapter 20

LINDY CHECKS HER notebook. "Bud and Melissa Reinhold, Brentwood, Tennessee. Daughter's name is Jenny. She's nineteen, a psych major, cute girl. Family's loaded."

"When do we strike?"

"According to Facebook, Jenny's coming home next weekend, so...how does next Friday sound?"

"Like music," he says. "Can I ask you a question? How come your notebook's called *Every Last Dime*?"

"Because that's how much we're gonna get from our victims."

He laughs.

Lindy stares at him a long time, then looks at the twins and says, "Guys? I need to tell you something: last week Keller asked me out on a date."

They give him a harsh look.

He shrugs, unsure where this is going, or why.

Lindy says, "I'm telling you because I don't want there to be any secrets between us from now on." She pauses. "I told him no. Then, on Saturday, he said some very ugly things to me, and I said if he felt that way why did he ask me out in the first place. And he said—"

She looks at Keller. "Do you remember what you said?"

"I was pissed. I didn't mean it."

Rayburn says, "What did you say, man?"

Keller sighs. "I said I asked her out because I wanted to fuck her, but I never liked her."

Claiburn starts to rise from his chair with evil intentions, but Lindy motions him to sit.

"It's all right," she says. "He didn't mean it. I also said some things to him I'm not proud of." She turns to Keller. "Your words really hurt me, but I forgive you."

"I'm really sorry, Lindy."

"I know. Thank you."

She says, "I know you're not dating anyone right now." She looks at the twins. "How about you guys?"

"What do you mean?" Rayburn says.

"Are you guys seeing anyone special?"

Keller sniggers.

"Not at the moment."

"Why are you asking?" Claiburn says.

"I was thinking maybe we should consider dating."

"You and who?"

"All of you."

Chapter 21

EACH OF THEM says it differently, but the consensus is "Hell Yes!"

Lindy says, "I need to think it through first, since it could create jealousy and gossip. But I'm willing to put it on the table." She pauses. "As a possibility." She pauses again. "For someday."

"Someday soon?" Keller asks, hopefully.

"I'd like that. If I can work it out in my head first. But I don't want to be pressured about it, okay? And I don't want you talking to each other about it behind my back. If it happens, it happens. But I don't want to be talked about or leered at."

They agree she's being more than reasonable.

Lindy briefs them on the Reinhold job, then says, "I appreciate the trust you've given me to make the decisions for the group. I've been doing a lot of research, and since we've made the conscious decision to engage in full-fledged criminal behavior, I think we need to do as much planning as possible. So if you guys are available, I'd like us to meet tomorrow evening for a dress rehearsal."

Keller laughs. "You mean a walk-through."

The twins smile.

Lindy grins. "Sorry. TME."

"What's that?"

"Too much estrogen?"

"Estrogen's cool," Claiburn says. "If you're a chick."

"Well, clearly I am, since you keep staring at my boobs."

He instantly averts his eyes.

"It's okay," she says. "I was just messin' with ya."

Since Keller's the only one that has his own place, they agree to meet at his apartment the next evening. With that settled they stand, and she forces herself not to smile at the wet spots on their crotches. No sense embarrassing her best friends in the world, the guys who will literally do anything for her from now on.

Chapter 22

LINDY STARTS THE meeting by outlining her plan. If Jenny and her parents go out Friday night, the guys will "pull a Wilcox," meaning Claiburn will follow them and report back to the others. When the family heads home, Keller and Rayburn will hide by the garage and follow the car inside, then pull their guns and terrify the family.

Second possibility: if Jenny goes out with her friends, and her parents (Bud and Melissa) stay home, they'll "pull a Lindy," meaning when Jenny leaves, the guys will ring the doorbell, and force their way inside when Bud or Melissa answers, as they did when invading Lindy's house.

After the guys demonstrate their roles, Lindy says: "As it turns out we picked an excellent crime vehicle, but we're not alone. There are nearly 6,000 home burglaries committed every day. And that's a good thing."

"Why?" Claiburn says.

"Because we can learn from their mistakes." She checks her notes. "Sixty percent use forced entry, like us. I couldn't find what 10% of them do, but you won't believe how a whopping 30% gain entry."

"With a key?"

She grins. "Nope, but good for you! I think you just explained the 10% I couldn't figure out!"

Claiburn beams.

"Believe it or not," she says, "Thirty percent of all burglars gain entry through an unlocked door or window. So if the Reinholds and Jenny go out Friday night, you and Rayburn can check the doors and windows while Keller follows them around town."

"If we find something open," Rayburn says, "we should go in?"

"Absolutely! That would give you hours to search the house. You should put some basic tools in your backpacks like a hammer and chisel in case you find a small safe you can bust into."

"What if they've got an alarm?"

"I'm sure they do, but I doubt they'll set it because Jenny's home for the weekend. She'll be in and out and they'll be rushing around. They won't be thinking about a break in."

"And if they *do* set it?"

"If they do, you'll know instantly. If the alarm goes off, haul your asses!"

"What if it's a silent alarm?"

"In that case, Keller and I will come visit you in prison."

"Not funny!" Rayburn says.

"If you're worried about a silent alarm, leave the house and drive around the neighborhood for 30 minutes and see if any cops show up. If not, go back in."

"Cool."

"Here's something else," Lindy says, reading her notes; "According to the FBI, the average home invader steals $2,185 worth of stuff, including guns, electronics and other stuff we don't want. Remember why we don't want those things?"

"Because you can't trust fences."

"That's right. Only 13% of home invaders get caught, but the ones that do made one of four mistakes: one, they didn't wear a mask; two, they left DNA at the scene; three, they tried to pawn their stolen goods too soon; or four, they were turned in by their fence or someone in their crew."

Rayburn says, "The problem with just taking cash and coins, most people don't keep much cash at their homes, and almost no one has gold or silver coins. I don't think it's worth the risk if we're only taking one piece of jewelry."

"I agree."

"You do?"

"Yes. At first, I didn't want to steal jewelry, because it's easy for cops to identify at pawn shops or on Craig's List or eBay. But then I learned it's not the jewelry that gets thieves in trouble, it's their lack of patience. A high percentage of crooks pawn their stolen goods at the nearest pawn shop, within a day after the robbery!"

Keller shakes his head. "How can anyone be that stupid?"

Lindy says, "They're usually drug addicts, desperate for cash. Fifty-eight percent of all robbers break into houses hoping to find illegal or prescription drugs."

Rayburn says, "If we take jewelry, how long do we have to wait before pawning it?"

"That's the best part: if we remove the diamonds from the cheaper pieces and sell them individually we can cash in immediately. But we'll only get about 20 cents on the dollar. Still, it's worth doing. We'll also want to grab everything that's real gold or silver, like bracelets, necklaces, rings, and earrings. If they're real, but nondescript, we'll be able to resell them without fear. As for the exquisite jewelry, if we want to get the maximum, we'll need to wait several years, until the police and insurance companies have forgotten about them. If we have the patience to sit on the finest pieces for several years, someday we'll be able to take a nice vacation together visiting pawn shops all over the country, each of us pawning a piece in each city. That gives us years to obtain and establish fake ID's, since the pawn shops will ask for our identities before paying us."

"Where will we keep the good stuff?" Keller asks.

"We'll split it up after each robbery and put them in safe deposit boxes at various banks. But remember, never get it appraised. Too dangerous. As for gold and silver coins, we should wait two years and unload them the same way: a few at a time, in different cities. We can spend the cash immediately, though I'd love to see us start a small business together so we can launder the money."

"How would that work?"

"We'd run the cash through the business and pay ourselves a salary and bonuses."

"We'd have to pay taxes on it!" Rayburn complains.

"True, but if you show up one day with beautiful new Jaguars, how are you gonna explain them to your dad?"

"Good point."

"So we'll take cash, gold, silver, and expensive jewelry."

"A lot of people have fake diamonds," Keller says. "How will we know the difference?"

She smiles. "I'm gonna teach you."

Claiburn frowns. "That sounds like a lot of work."

"Really? Gosh, I thought you'd enjoy the extra time with me."

"Well...I mean, I would like the extra time with you, but...Ray and me are muscle. Keller's the one who searches the houses with the daughters."

"True. But what if Keller's following the family and you and Rayburn find an open door? You'd have hours to search for the good stuff, and you'd be able to load it up and get away without having to confront the family."

"I'm not great at learning stuff."

"Like I said, I'll work with you."

"I like it," Keller says. "We could've made a fortune if we'd taken all we could have from the Wilcoxes."

"Yes," Lindy says. "But we're learning as we go."

"Kim had a shitload of jewelry," Keller says.

"I'm sure she did."

"If you'd just let us take it in the first place, we—"

Claiburn interrupts: "Let it go, Shithead. She already said—"

Lindy raises her hand. "Guys. Please."

They look at her. "Two things," she says. "First, let's not ever argue among ourselves. We're family now. We need to support each other. And second, there's no rule that says we can't go back and get Kim's jewelry another time."

They like the sound of that.

Lindy says, "Are we good?"

They nod.

"Thank you. I really want us to be close. And to prove it, I'd like to give each of you a kiss for good luck."

"On the mouth?" Claiburn says.

"Of course. I'm not your granny, after all."

They line up. Claiburn says, "Can we kiss in private?"

"I think that's a good idea. How about I stand in the hallway, and you guys come out one at a time?"

They do, and she makes them happy they did. After giving each of them equivalent kisses—which she correctly assumes are the best of their lives—she rejoins them and says, "Remember, we're a team, and I'm not a possession, so there can't be any jealousy." She looks at each of them, but allows her eyes to linger on Claiburn as she says, "Because if there is, we'll have to stop. And that would be a shame."

Chapter 23

Saturday, 4:00 p.m.

"WHAT'S THIS?" KELLER says, looking around.

"Our new business," Lindy says. "If you're interested."

"And if we're not?"

"I'll do it myself."

"I'm in," Claiburn says.

She smiles. "Thank you."

"What type of business is it going to be?" Rayburn asks.

"An online reseller."

"What's that?"

"Customers bring us items they want to sell online, and we'll take photos, write a sales pitch, and post them to various sites, like eBay. When they sell, we keep 20% for our trouble."

"Why don't they do it themselves?"

"Most people can't be bothered. They don't know how, and don't want to take the time to learn. It's a lot easier to bring us their stuff and let us sell it for them."

"Who pays for shipping?"

"The buyers."

Keller snorts. "Sounds like work."

Lindy smiles. "I'll do the lion's share."

"Which is what, exactly?"

She cocks her head. "You mean in addition to coming up with the idea, finding the place, negotiating the lease, designing the build out, and paying the first month out of my own pocket?"

He grins. "Yeah. In addition to all that."

"I'll work the front desk, answer the phone, deal with the customers...shall I continue?"

He smirks. "Please do."

"I'll do all the copywriting, the advertising, the photographing. I'll post the ads online, maintain a regular social media presence, respond to the emails, customer comments and complaints, I'll—"

"Stop!" Rayburn says. "You're giving me a headache."

Claiburn says, "What would *we* have to do?"

"Go to the customer's homes or businesses to pick up the large or heavy items they want us to sell, move the heavy stuff around for me here at the store, pack the sold items in boxes, take it to UPS for shipping...that sort of stuff."

"In other words, the grunt work," Keller says.

"I prefer to call it packing and shipping."

"Sure you would. But it's loading dock stuff."

"I won't disagree. Then again, I'm not pushing this on you. If you're not interested, I'll find someone else."

"I'll do it," Claiburn says.

"Of course you will!" Keller says.

Lindy gives him a look, then makes a sweeping gesture with her hand and says, "This will be our display area. Our show room. It's where we'll set up the new stuff to make it super inviting."

"What new stuff?"

"I'm gonna buy some merchandise we can sell or trade to walk-in traffic. And if we don't sell it, no problem. It'll serve our purpose."

"Which is what?"

"To make us look elegant and classy."

"This whole operation could be run out of your home," Rayburn says.

"True. But I'm looking at the big picture."

"Which is what?"

"We can launder a substantial amount of money through this shop, like the loose diamonds and simple gold and silver bracelets and earrings that can't be traced. And eventually we'll sell the gold and silver coins we've been saving."

Claiburn looks hurt. "I thought we were gonna pawn all that stuff in a few years when we take our vacation together."

"I'd still like to do that. But there's only so many items we can pawn without raising people's suspicions. And if what you guys collected last night from the Reinholds is any indication, we'll soon be drowning in jewelry."

The guys smile, proud of their recent haul. She won't burst their bubble by telling them 95% of the stuff they took was costume jewelry, and that what they believe to be diamonds are actually rhinestones. She'll save that for the next meeting, where she can gracefully point out the difference between paste and prime jewelry. By then, their minds will be on the next job instead of the last one, and they'll be less defensive and more responsive to constructive criticism.

Keller says, "This place is awfully small. I doubt you can store very much. You're gonna outgrow it within weeks."

She produces a key from her jeans pocket.

"What's that?" he says.

"The key to our storage facility. That's where you'll haul the big stuff while we wait for it to sell."

"How far is that from here?"

"About a mile. I'll show you, if you're interested."

"No rush. You probably won't even be open for several months."

"Actually, there's very little to do: the landlord's gonna paint, build in a desk and countertop, and put in some carpeting. He said if I choose a carpet that's in stock he can have it ready to go in three weeks."

"How much would it cost us to go in with you?"

"The start-up cost is thirty grand, and that includes twenty thousand for the display items. Your shares would be seventy-five hundred each, if you're interested."

Rayburn says, "So it's basically this open room with a desk and countertop, and an office and bathroom in the back?"

"Pretty much. Except we won't be using the back room as an office."

"Why not?"

"I thought I'd put a bed in there."

"For what?"

She winks. "What do you think?"

"I'm in!" Keller says.

"Me too!" Rayburn says.

"I was already in," Claiburn says. "Even before you said that."

"Yes you were," she coos, while casting a look of triumph at Keller and Rayburn that dares them to roll their eyes.

Chapter 24

ACCORDING TO THE guys, last night's home invasion went perfectly. But she couldn't help noticing whenever she asked a detailed question they looked at each other before one of them—usually Keller—responded. And though Claiburn is quiet by nature, he spoke not a word throughout the entire briefing, which gave her concern at the time, and still does.

Last night yielded a disappointing result: $96 in cash and change.

Change? she thinks. *Are you kidding me?* Since when do thieves have to rely on penny jars?

It's not like the Reinholds are a mystery family. True, she's never been in Jenny's house, but she knows they've got enough money to live in Brentwood, arguably the most exclusive neighborhood in all of Nashville. So they collected three pounds of costume jewelry and two 10-year-old his and her Rolex watches and a single Cartier bangle that retails for $6,300 new. Seriously? No collections? No gold and silver bangles and baubles? No safe?

Doesn't make sense.

"What about the jewelry Bud and Melissa were wearing?" she asked during their briefing earlier today at Keller's apartment.

"They told us they don't wear watches," Keller said. "If they want to know what time it is they check their cell phones."

"Wedding bands?"

"Plain gold. Melissa's was gold, too. Not worth much. I decided to let them keep those."

"No diamond engagement ring?"

"According to Melissa and Jenny she lost it years ago."

Because Jenny Reinhold's a decent person, Lindy told the guys to threaten her in front of the parents, but not to shove her around. Keller said that part went well, and he did the panty thing, which he claims he and the twins have perfected. But when Lindy asked for them he turned them over with great reluctance. She couldn't care less about Jenny's panties, but it was too gross thinking why he might want to keep them. He claimed they were a souvenir, but Lindy pointed out perverts take souvenirs, not professional burglars.

So the guys split the cash with Lindy and gave her the jewelry to hold. At the time, something about the costume jewelry bothered her. Something she couldn't quite put her finger on. But now, studying each piece carefully, it's obvious what happened.

She calls Rayburn's cell phone. When he answers she asks, "Are you with Claiburn?"

"Yeah. What's up?"

"I need to ask you something privately. Can you make up an excuse and ditch him and call me back?"

"Sure."

"Thanks."

Five minutes later, Rayburn calls.

Lindy says, "Are you alone?"

"Yeah. What's up?"

"Stay put. I'll call you back in two minutes."

She hangs up and calls Claiburn. When he answers she says, "I need to ask you something."

"What?"

"This is just between you and me, okay?"

"Okay."

"Can I trust you?"

"Yes."

"You swear?"

"Yes." He pauses. "Why? What's wrong?"

"I'm a girl."

He holds the phone away from his ear, looks at it a moment, shakes his head, then puts it back to his ear and says, "I already knew that."

"Right. But girls and guys are different in a million ways. And one of those ways is we know a lot about jewelry."

He says nothing, so she continues: "At noon today I looked at the bag Keller gave me and knew immediately it was costume jewelry. I didn't want to say anything because I didn't' want to hurt anyone's feelings. But now I think you guys knew all along it was costume jewelry."

She waits a few moments to let her words sink in. Of the three, he's the one who's truly smitten with her. She pictures him squirming, wanting to come forward, but not wanting to go against his brother and Keller. So she says, "I don't want to get you in trouble with the others, so I'll make you this promise: if you tell me what really happened last night, I won't confront Rayburn or Keller. It'll be our secret."

"I thought we weren't supposed to have secrets from each other."

"We're not. But I think you and the guys are keeping one from me. About last night."

"What secret is that?"

Chapter 25

LINDY SAYS, "I think you guys got a lot more than ninety-six dollars in cash last night. I also think you got some very nice pieces of jewelry. I think Keller and Rayburn took the bulk of that cash to a local department store this morning and used it to buy a bunch of costume jewelry which Keller put in a bag and gave to me at noon. I think you guys kept the nicest jewelry and only turned over two clunky watches and a Cartier bracelet. Am I wrong?"

"Why would you think *that*?"

"This costume jewelry is brand new. It's never been worn."

"How can you *say* that? The pieces are all scratched. I *saw* the scratches."

Lindy thinking: *Of course you did. But what you can't see is my smile, though it's not a happy one.*

"Claiburn?"

"Yeah?"

"I'm a girl, remember?"

"Why do you keep *saying* that?"

"Because you guys took your keys or some other object and scuffed the jewelry up to try to fool me. But you didn't take into account the fading."

"What's that?"

"When a woman wears costume jewelry, like a bracelet or ring, the moisture from her skin causes the alloys to tarnish and stain. I'm looking at the underside of these rings and bracelets, and the gold and silver plating on the earrings where they should have made contact with the skin, and guess what: there's no fading and no spots."

"Maybe Melissa takes really good care of her jewelry. Maybe she polishes it, or puts something on it to—"

She interrupts: "This is brand new costume jewelry, Claiburn, and you *know* it. And the fact you still haven't admitted it breaks my heart. I wouldn't put it past the others to cheat me, but I had special feelings for you. I thought you had my back."

"I do."

"You guys begged me for another chance and I gave it to you. And now, only a couple of days later, you've already screwed me. And here I thought we had something special."

"We do."

"Clearly we don't."

"It was their idea, not mine."

She goes silent.

He says, "I wanted what *you* wanted: everyone to be honest and get along. But...they think you're play-acting. They need your contacts and ideas, but they want to get as much cash as possible in the shortest amount of time. They want to fence the jewelry. And also..."

"Also what?"

"You need to be careful with your notebook."

"And why is that?"

"The guys want to steal it."

"I see. Thanks for telling me."

"Are you and me cool now?"

"We are. But I'm sure as hell not gonna have sex with you guys."

"Why not *me*? I told you the truth just now."

"No you didn't, Claiburn. You *admitted* the truth, but only after I confronted you about the lie. That's a big difference. It shows me you're better than they are, but it also shows you don't have my back. It shows I can't trust you the way I thought I could. And I could never make love to someone I can't trust."

"I was against it from the start. I told them it wouldn't work. I told them they were fucking up the greatest thing we ever had."

"You told them it wouldn't work?"

"Yes."

"Well that's hardly taking my side. You should have told them it wasn't right. You should have refused to be a part of it. You should have told them I've been working my ass off to make sure everything went smoothly."

"I'm sorry, Lindy."

"Me too, Claiburn."

"What can I do to make it up?"

"I'm not sure. Probably nothing."

"What if I kill them?"

"Excuse me?"

Chapter 26

CLAIBURN SAYS, "I *did* tell them it wasn't right to steal the jewelry. But they did it anyway. And I couldn't tell you because I knew you'd kick us all out of the group and I'd lose you forever. And I can't let that happen, Lindy. I can't lose you. I'd do anything for you."

"Did you just say you'd kill Keller and your own twin brother?"

"Yes. And I meant it. Just say the word. I'll kill them and we'll find two other guys."

"Well, obviously I would never tell you to do that. But I'm impressed you tossed it out there."

"What can I do to make it up to you?"

"I'm not sure. But I agree, there needs to be something. I'll think it over. Can you call me back in thirty minutes?"

"Yes."

"Claiburn?"

"Yeah?"

"I'm the one who called Rayburn a few minutes ago. I told him to separate himself from you and call me back. When he did I told him to wait a few minutes, so now I'm gonna call him back. But I only did that so I could talk to you. I'm telling you this so you'll know I'm not playing you against each other."

"I wouldn't think that in the first place. What will you say when you call him back?"

"I don't know. I'll make up something. But don't tell him we talked. And be sure to erase this call from your phone."

"Okay. Thanks, Lindy."

After ending the call, she finds herself dreading the next one, because Rayburn's a snake. She wracks her brain thinking of a strong reason to speak privately. What can she possibly say to him in private that she couldn't say in front of Claiburn? What could she possibly *ask* him—

And then it comes to her.

She dials his number. He answers with: "Took you long enough."

"Sorry. My dad walked in on me."

"At the new store?"

"Yeah."

"Why?"

"He's excited for me. He wanted to see it."

"Why?"

Lindy takes a deep breath. "Because he loves me. And because he personally guaranteed my lease."

"Ah. Well *that* makes sense. What did you want to tell me?"

"I'm concerned about Claiburn."

"Why?"

"I sensed he's getting romantic feelings for me."

He laughs. "You *sensed* that, did you?"

"Yes. Do you think it's gonna be an issue?"

"Of course. He's a nut job. He's hopelessly in love with you. He'd marry you right now if you asked."

"How big a problem will it be?"

"That's up to you. This whole thing about how you might fuck us? Don't get me wrong, I'm all for it. But you're asking for trouble."

"So I should back off?"

"No."

"Why not?"

"Because Keller and Claiburn actually believe your bullshit. They're falling all over themselves waiting to climb into your non-existent bed. You can get them to do all kinds of shit by holding that promise over their heads."

"Is that what you think I've been doing?"

"It couldn't be more obvious."

"Why do you think that? It's not true, by the way."

"Of course it is. And the reason is just as obvious: you're smart and ridiculously pretty. You could get an acting job on looks alone, which is a damn good thing, because your acting skills leave a lot to be desired. The rest of us are decent actors, but no one on earth would mistake us for leading men. I mean, Keller's an unemployed psychopath, and me and Clay are 22 years old, unemployed, live in our father's basement, and share a shitty car with bald tires and a single hubcap."

"Just so you know, I would have been willing to do everything I said. Not to *use* you, but to keep the group tight."

"If you say so. But I notice you put it in past tenths just now. Why the sudden change?"

"It's not worth it. It'll cause problems."

"Why?"

"Like you said: Claiburn's in love, Keller's a psychopath, and you think the whole thing was a ruse to control your actions."

"Fine. Do what you want. Who cares?"

"Thanks for your input."

"Whatever."

They hang up and she dials a number. Jackie Keck answers with: "Let me guess: you need another favor."

"If you're available."

"When?"

"Immediately."

"Here in town?"

"Yup."

"Who do I have to fuck?"

Lindy pauses. "You'd *do* that?"

Jackie laughs. "I said that for Bill's benefit. He's sitting ten feet from me, eavesdropping. What's the job?"

"Driving and waiting."

"How long?"

"Two hours, tops."

"What's it pay?"

"How does a hundred bucks sound?"

"Like a down payment on two hundred."

Lindy laughs.

After working out the details Lindy barely has time to catch her breath before her phone rings.

"It's me," Claiburn says.

She checks the time. Thirty minutes. On the dot. Good sign.

"You and Rayburn share a car, right?"

"Uh huh."

"You think he'll let you have it for a few hours tonight?"

"He won't have a choice in the matter."

"Good. You know the Devonshire Hotel? The one by the outdoor mall?"

"Yeah. Wait. Is that the one with the big courtyard or the one behind the office store?"

"The courtyard."

"Yeah. I know it."

"Could you meet me there tonight at eight?"

"Of course."

"When you get to the parking lot, call me and I'll tell you what room I'm in."

"Is it just the two of us?"

"Yes. But we're just going to talk, okay?"

"Okay."

"For now. But if things go super well…"

"Yeah?"

"We'll see."

"I'll do whatever you say." He pauses. "I really mean it, Lindy. If you want someone's head cut off, or their nuts on a silver platter, just tell me and I'll do it. I'll do it on the way there if you want. Just say the word."

Lindy stares at her phone in horror. Not knowing quite how to respond to his offer of bringing fresh body parts to their date she simply says, "Thank you, Claiburn. That won't be necessary."

"Okay. But if you change your mind—"

"Right. If I do, I'll let you know. See you at eight."

Chapter 27

RAYBURN CALLS KELLER and says, "Something's up."

"What do you mean?"

"Clay's taking a shower."

"So?"

"*So?* My brother's taking a shower! At night! And he wants to use the car."

"Are you saying he's got a date?"

"I only know he's meeting someone."

"Who's the lucky girl?"

"Best guess? Lindy Bissel."

"*What?* No way! He *told* you that?"

"No, of course not."

"Then how do you know?"

"She's the only one on his radar. He's head over heels in love with her."

"You think he's planning to *kidnap* her? We should warn her!"

Rayburn winces at Keller's stupidity. Then says: "I think she asked him out."

"Why the fuck would she do that?" He pauses. "Whoa! You think she's gonna *fuck* him? Why *him?* I mean, no offense to your brother, it's just...I thought she'd pick me first. I was the first one to ask her out."

"Calm down. This isn't a booty call. I think we fucked up."

"What do you mean?"

"We should have given her half the jewelry, not the three shittiest pieces."

"You think Clay told her?"

"No, but I think she's smart enough to figure it out. Remember how she kept staring at the fake stuff today? Like she didn't believe our story?"

"Nope. But if you're right, why would she ask Clay out on a date?"

"Again, it's not a date, though *he* probably thinks it is. I'm guessing she's going to ask him about last night. It'll probably take him ten seconds to spill his guts."

"Tell him not to."

"Right. Tell Clay not to cave in to the woman he loves. Good luck with that."

"What should we do?"

"Follow him. I mean, it's possible I'm wrong. Then again, he's taking a shower. And moaning."

"Moaning?"

"It's something he does when he's excited."

"I'm on my way."

Chapter 28

AT PRECISELY EIGHT o'clock, Claiburn pulls into the parking lot of the Devonshire Hotel and calls Lindy to get the room number, which turns out to be 316. He grabs his duffel, heads to the lobby, and catches the elevator. When she opens the door she shows him a big smile and says, "I'm so happy you came!"

He enters the room, closes the door behind him. "Of course I came. I'd travel 100% around the world to meet you."

Lindy chooses not to explain that if he traveled 100% around the world to meet her he'd be right back where he started, in which case he'd still have to travel to the hotel. Instead, she says: "Thanks, Claiburn. I believe you. What's in the duffel?"

"Guess!"

She eyes the bag warily. Surely he didn't cut someone's...

He sets it on the floor, unzips the top, then picks it up and turns it upside down so the contents spill out on the bed.

Lindy watches him the same way people watch highway accidents: with a combination of curiosity and dread. But it turns out to be his share of all the loot they've acquired.

"It's for you," he says.

"No. It wouldn't be right."

"I love you, Lindy. I want you to have it."

She looks at the bounty: 25 Morgan silver dollars, 10 Krugerrands, and... "Is that the jewelry they gave you from last night?"

He nods, and sits beside her on the bed. "Keller and Ray kept the best pieces."

"Are you sure about that? Because these are insanely nice."

"I'm sure. But I didn't care. I didn't want any of it if they weren't gonna share it with you."

She looks into his eyes. "I can't believe you're so sweet."

She also can't believe the two pieces of jewelry. Lindy's no expert, but she's guessing the ring and bracelet together would retail for a quarter mill. She wonders what the better pieces are worth.

"These were in a safe?"

"Uh huh."

"So they lied about that?"

He looks down. "They lied about everything."

"Tell me."

He bites his lip. "I...can't."

"It's okay." She puts her hand on his knee and asks, "Do you really want me to have all this?"

"Yes. I'll be upset if you don't accept it."

"Well...okay. But it's exceedingly generous of you, and I should give you something valuable in return." She leans toward him and tenderly kisses his lips. "What can I do to make you happy?"

"Can I ask for anything?"

She cocks her head. "Anything within reason."

He says, "I'd like you to not have sex with Ray or Keller."

"Very well," she says. "I promise."

"And you can't kiss them, either. Not even for good luck."

She smiles. "Fair enough. Anything else?"

His face turns bright red.

She says, "Was there something else?"

"I don't want you to get mad."

"It's okay. I might say no, but I won't get mad."

"Could I—um...could I touch your boobs?"

She smiles. "You can do a lot more than that, Claiburn."

"Really?"

"A *lot* more."

And so he does.

Chapter 29

BEFORE LEAVING, CLAIBURN puts all her loot in the duffel and asks if she wants him to carry it to her car. She tells him no, she can manage, then kisses him goodbye. Then she puts on her long black wig and her newest addition: fake glasses, then checks herself in the mirror, and places a call. When Jackie answers, Lindy says, "Where are you?"

"At the mall."

"You're *shopping?*"

"Nope. Just sitting in my car, waiting for your call. You ready to go?"

"I am."

"Okay. I'll be there in less than a minute. Want me to park out back?"

"Yes please."

Thirty seconds later Jackie calls. "Are you outside yet?"

"Almost."

"Stay inside till I tell you to come out."

"Why?"

"Just do it. And when I come, be ready to run!"

"What on earth?"

"I'll call you soon. Just be ready."

Thirty seconds pass, then her phone rings. "Okay, I'm here," Jackie says. "*Run!*"

Lindy races as fast as she can while carrying the duffel. She jumps inside, and Jackie guns the engine and roars out of the parking lot.

"What the hell's *happening?*" Lindy asks.

"Two guys are beating someone to death."

"Where?"

"Far side of the hotel. It's awful. I think they killed him."

Lindy's mind goes to Claiburn. *Has* to be him. Rayburn and Keller must have followed him in Keller's car. When Claiburn came out they confronted him, and attacked.

She starts bawling.

Jackie says, "It's okay, baby. I'm sorry. I didn't mean to scare you."

She keeps talking, but nothing she says can make Lindy stop. She cries all the way to her store, where they left her car.

"I won't leave you like this," Jackie said.

"Th-thank you." She does that huffing thing, like kids do after a long, hard cry.

"Lindy: tell me what's troubling you."

That's not going to happen. Lindy's not about to tell her that two of her associates just beat her other associate to death—the one she had sex with just minutes ago—and that now they'll be coming for her.

"I—I can't go home tonight."

"No problem, honey. You can stay with us."

"No. I'll get a room somewhere."

"Are you in trouble?"

"Yes."

"How can I help?"

"Give me a sec." Lindy's thoughts are flying in all directions, like a giant rope unravelling into a million threads at warp speed. She needs to grab one of the threads and hold on for dear life. Focus on that one, then gather the others, one at a time. Because if ever she needed to get it exactly right, this is the time. Any mistake in the next half hour, no matter how small, could lead to prison...or death.

Okay, slow it down. Start with...

Rayburn and Keller. They either killed Claiburn or nearly killed him. If they nearly killed him they're probably taking him to a hospital right now. But if they killed him they'll...

They'll be looking for her.

And where will they look?

Three places: the hotel, her new store—where she is right now—or her house. But they'll start with the hotel, if Claiburn told them the room number. And surely he did.

Lindy huffs a couple more times, then her breath catches in her throat. Finally she asks: "You saw the two guys, but did they see *you?*"

"I don't think so."

"We need to be certain."

Lindy's phone rings.

It's Rayburn.

She waits till it stops ringing, then waits for the beep that says he's left a message.

Jackie says, "I'm sure they heard us leave the parking lot just now, but the building was between us, so no, they didn't see me or my car."

"What about when you first pulled in? That's when you called me."

The phone beeps.

Jackie says, "You sound better. Are you okay?"

"I think so."

"Good. When I first pulled in I had my window down. I heard the screams from a good distance away, and immediately cut my lights. Then I called you, and backed slowly out of the parking lot. By then I was too far away for them to see my car or license plate, and there were lots of parked cars between us anyway. I drove around the back way, turned the car around, then called you to come running."

She thinks a moment, then nods her head. "They didn't see me. I'm positive."

Lindy presses the button that plays the phone messages and hears an out-of-breath Rayburn doing his best to sound casual: "Hey, Lindy, it's Rayburn. Give me a call when you get this. I need to talk to you. It's really important."

She erases the message and asks, "Did you see anyone else milling about the parking lot?"

"No. Despite all the cars, the place was quiet. That doesn't mean no one saw them, it only means *I* didn't see anyone else."

"Okay. Good job. So here's the plan: I want you to drive to your house and wait for me. I'm gonna grab some stuff from my house and bring it to you."

"What kind of stuff?"

"You don't want to know. But everything I'm bringing will fit into this duffel bag. And I want you to keep it for me, and I want you to promise not to look inside, no matter what. And you can't let Bill or anyone else look in it."

"Sure. No problem."

"*Promise* me!"

"Right. Well, I don't want to sound insensitive in your time of crisis, but—"

"I'll give you ten thousand dollars."

"I'll guard it with my life."

"And you won't let anyone look inside?"

"For ten grand you could zip my nephew in the bag, and I'd let him cry till he suffocates."

"Thank you. Because once you see it, you can't un-see it, if you know what I mean."

"I don't have a clue what you mean, and nor do I want to know."

"After I drop the bag off, I'll get a hotel room for the night, and possibly several days. But I need Bill to make a call using my cell phone."

"To who?"

"I'll tell you when I get to your place." Lindy goes quiet. Just sits there, staring into space.

"What's wrong?"

She says nothing, but even in the dark car Jackie can see she's worried. Lindy's phone rings again. And keeps ringing.

"You're *scaring* me!" Jackie says. "What's going on?" She follows Lindy's gaze. "Is it that car? The Dodge Charger?"

Lindy nods as if in slow motion.

"What about it?"

"I think it's them. Do you have a gun?"

"No I don't have a fucking gun! Jesus, Lindy! What the hell have you gotten me into?"

Chapter 30

LINDY WATCHES FOR several seconds, then breathes a sigh of relief. "Same car, different color. It's not them."

"Thank God!" Jackie says. "Who are we talking about, the guys that beat up the other guy?"

"Yeah."

By now her phone has stopped ringing. This time Keller left the message: "Lindy, we need to talk to you. It's urgent. The police just called Rayburn's dad. They said someone killed Claiburn tonight. Jesus, Lindy! The police are gonna be crawling all over us. Call me. *Please!*"

Something about his voice. She's not convinced. He's probably trying to lure her someplace. She erases the message.

Jackie says, "Will you at least tell me what the right color is?"

"Huh?"

"The Dodge Charger. What's the color I'm supposed to worry about?"

"I'd rather not say. I don't want to frighten you."

"Are you kidding me? I'm already sitting in a pint of my own piss."

Lindy looks at her. "Really?"

"Let's not forget I'm twice your age. And just so you know, if that car *had* been the right color, I'd be sitting in a lot more than piss."

"Hopefully that won't happen. Let's get moving."

"You don't have to tell me twice. As Lindy opens the door to get out, Jackie says, "Are your parents at home right now?"

"Probably."

"Would they find it odd you're wearing a black wig?"

Lindy instinctively looks at her reflection in the rear-view mirror. The glasses must have fallen off in the hotel parking lot when she ran to the car, but she completely forgot about the wig. She pulls it off, smooths her hair. "Thanks, Jackie."

"No sweat. See you later. And be careful!"

As soon as Jackie closes the door, Lindy steps on the gas and goes straight home. Naturally Mom and Dad want to talk.

"Slow down, kiddo!" Dad says. "How's the new place coming along?"

"Wonderful. Can't wait to show it to you."

"When will that happen?"

"Three weeks."

He frowns. "Not before?"

"Actually, they haven't started the renovation yet."

"I thought you said it was going wonderfully."

"It is. I meant they're ready to start. Um...I need to run."

"Where are you going?"

"I'm driving to Lexington for a couple of days."

"*Lexington?* Why? And not at night I hope."

"I'll be fine. They've got a reselling store there, and I want to talk to the owner."

"I must say, you're taking this new store very seriously! I'm proud of you, kiddo!"

"Thanks Dad."

"That Lexington store's open on Sundays?" Mom asks.

"I think so. But if not, I'll stay till Monday."

"You should look them up online and check their hours of operation. If they're not open tomorrow, you can stay home and drive there on Monday."

"It's only an hour. And don't forget, I've got friends at UK. I'll be fine."

Her mom frowns. "Where'd you get the duffel bag?"

"You like it?"

"No. It's old and filthy."

"Maybe that's why it only cost five bucks."

"You overpaid."

"Thanks Mom."

"Need some help packing?"

"Nope. I'm fine."

Keller and Rayburn will check the new store first, then drive here, so she's only got minutes to get away. Problem is, her mom's looking over her shoulder, trying to carry on a conversation, and Lindy needs to climb under her desk and pull the baseboard loose to get her cash and coins.

Finally, her mom leaves the room, and Lindy grabs her stash and puts it into the duffel. Then she runs through the den, gives her parents a hug and tells them she loves them. At the last minute she realizes her mom intends to walk her to her car and that won't do, since she'll linger.

"Mom. Please. I'm fine. Sit down."

"Well..."

"Please. I'm fine." She guides her mom to her chair and says, "Love you."

"In and out like a mosquito!" Mom says.

"Like a revolving door," Dad says.

Like a penis during sex, Lindy thinks, but doesn't say it. Instead, she rushes out the door before they can craft any other ways to impede her escape.

She drives to Jackie's house, rushes to the front door, rings the doorbell. When Jackie lets her in she places the duffel on the floor, hands Jackie her cell phone and says, "Got a pen and paper?"

Jackie hands her what she needs, and Lindy starts writing feverishly. After a few minutes she hands Jackie the paper and says, "The minute I leave, turn your TV on, and watch one of the local stations until they mention the man you saw getting beaten up at the hotel tonight. His name is Claiburn Foster. If they say he's dead, have Bill call 911 from this cell phone. Tell him to disguise his voice and read this message exactly as I wrote it, then hang up immediately. Tell him not to stay on the phone more than 15 seconds. Then have him take a sledge hammer and smash the phone into tiny pieces and flush them down the toilet."

"What if this Claiburn guy's not dead?"

"Then sit tight and wait for me to get in touch with you. But check the TV and Internet for news of his condition. He could die tomorrow, or the next day. And if he does, Bill needs to make that call. Oh, and tell him this phone might ring lots of times before he smashes it. But he can't answer it for any reason."

"Got it. What about the duffel bag?"

"Hide it. And no matter what happens—"

"Don't look inside, right? I got it."

Lindy rushes to her car and drives straight to Lexington, stops at a drug store, buys a "morning after" pill, and takes it. Then she gets a room and immediately starts charging her real phone. When it gets to 20% she calls her parents to tell them she arrived safely. Then she checks the Internet for Louisville news and sees the report: a young man was brutally murdered outside the Devonshire Hotel. It's just a headline at this point, and there's no story or details, but it's enough to make her rush to the toilet and vomit. She starts sobbing again, and continues crying while she washes her face, brushes her teeth, changes into her bedclothes. When she finally stops crying she lies down on the bed and thinks about Claiburn. Weird, moronic, sensitive, sweet, generous, loving Claiburn: a guy she barely knew, who proved to be the one man who loved her most.

Of course it wouldn't have worked. They were polar opposites. But he loved her, and would have cut his twin brother's nuts off for her, which is something most women can't say about their boyfriends. And he gave her gold, silver, and jewelry worth at least $80,000 in the aftermarket.

Lindy starts crying again. And when she's completely cried out, she starts replaying it in her mind: they undressed and had sex. He didn't have a condom, so after they finished she jumped in the shower and scrubbed down. He joined her—which annoyed her at the time—but since he'd given her shit load of money, how could she say no? And now she's glad he took that shower, because he's dead, and soon the police will have Keller and Rayburn in custody, and when they try to implicate Lindy in their criminal activities, at least the coroner won't find her DNA on Claiburn's body.

Then again, their mutual DNA is all over the bedsheets in Room 316 at the Devonshire Hotel...

Chapter 31

BACK IN LOUISVILLE, Bill's reluctant to call 911. He's quite fond of Lindy, but he'd rather not get involved in a homicide. On the other hand, ten grand will impact their lives in a meaningful way. So at Jackie's urging, after hearing about Claiburn's death, he dials 911 on Lindy's throwaway phone. When the operator answers, Bill reads: "I know you're recording this, so please don't interrupt. Tonight, two Louisville men, Ian Keller and Rayburn Foster, beat and killed Claiburn Foster in the parking lot of the Devonshire Hotel. Keller and Foster are responsible for the recent armed robbery of Bud and Melissa Reinhold, of Brentwood, Tennessee."

He hangs up and says, "How was that?"

"Ridiculous," Jackie says.

"How so?"

"You sounded like Peter O'Toole, in *Lawrence of Arabia*. Now hurry up and destroy the phone."

Chapter 32

LINDY SLEEPS SURPRISINGLY well, all things considered, and searches the Internet for the location of the local reseller, which turns out to be in a strip center. She drives there and spends a full hour talking to the owner, then walks to the Mexican restaurant two doors down, has lunch, and goes back to the hotel, where she hangs out, waiting for the police to call.

On Monday morning her dad calls and says he received a phone call in the middle of the night from the Jefferson County Jail. "They wanted to know if we would accept a call from Ian Keller. We said no. What's this about?"

"You're sure it was Ian Keller?"

"Yes. I wrote it down."

That's the news Lindy was waiting for. She tells her dad she has no idea why the guy from her acting class would call *her*, then checks out of the hotel, drives to Louisville, and goes straight to her bank, where she writes a check from her new company for $9,000, makes it payable to herself, and waits to be paid. After a few minutes the teller places a stack of fifties and twenties on the counter, and counts it twice, while Lindy watches. Then she places the money in an envelope and gives it to Lindy. Ten minutes later, Lindy knocks on Bill and Jackie's door. When Jackie opens it, she gives her a big hug.

"Does this mean you're safe?" Jackie says.

"I think so."

"Goody! Now pay me!"

She enters the house and says, "I need the duffel bag."

Jackie looks her straight in the face and says, "What duffel bag?"

Chapter 33

"OH MY GOD, look at your face!" Jackie says. "Relax. I was only making a joke."

"Not funny."

"Sorry. Give me a minute to fetch it. Want a soft drink? I've got Sprite or Diet Coke."

"No thanks."

As Lindy starts to take a seat, Bill enters the room. They make small talk till Jackie brings the duffel. Lindy says, "Give me a sec." She takes the duffel to their dining room table, unzips it, checks the contents, and says, "I appreciate everything you've done for me."

"How could we refuse?" Bill says. "Not only do you pay well, but you're Ashley's only friend these days."

"What he means is, you're like family to us," Jackie says, frowning at her husband.

Lindy gives them the bank envelope and adds a thousand dollars she still has from the Joe and Kim Wilcox heist. Then says, "You guys have always been great, so I don't want to impose any further. I still need someone to hold this duffel for a long time, but I have a friend who's glad to do it."

"Is it someone you trust more than us?" Jackie asks.

"No. But I do trust her, and she offered to do it for a thousand bucks."

She and Bill look at each other. He shakes his head. Jackie says, "That's not enough."

Lindy says, "Per month."

"Excuse me?"

"I offered my friend a thousand dollars a month to keep the duffel safe."

"What's the time frame?"

"Somewhere between 90 days and four years."

"We'll do it!" she says.

"What's in the duffel?" Bill asks.

Jackie says, "You don't want to know."

"Yes I do," Bill says.

"Clothes and makeup," Lindy says. "But they're special clothes, so please keep them in a safe place."

Bill says, "That's all I wanted to know. Thanks."

"I'll want to check them every month when I pay you."

"Of course."

Lindy drives home, pulls into her driveway, and sees two men standing on her porch. They turn and wave, then wait for her to enter the garage and come to the front door. When she does they identify themselves as police detectives Steve Emmert and John Wilson.

Wilson says, "And you're Lindy Bissel?

"Yes sir."

"May we join you?"

Chapter 34

"I GUESS SO," Lindy says. She backs up to let them enter. "What's this about?"

Wilson says, "May we sit down?"

"My mom would probably want us to sit in the den."

"Emmert says, "Are your parents home?"

"Nope, but Mom should be back in a half hour. Do you want to wait?"

"Can I ask how old you are?"

"Twenty-two."

"It's up to you, Lindy," Wilson says. "You're old enough to speak to us without your mom being present, but you're under no obligation to answer our questions."

Emmert quickly adds: "But it would be extremely helpful if you would."

She shrugs. "I'm willing to...I guess. What's this about?"

"We're investigating the death of a young man named Claiburn Foster. We understand he took acting classes with you at the community center. Did you know him?"

"Yes."

"How well?"

"I knew him and his brother. We were casual acquaintances. We worked together on a couple of skits."

"When did you hear the news about Claiburn's death?"

"I saw it on TV last night."

"And where were you at the time?"

"Lexington."

Emmert asks for details: why was she there, what time did she arrive, who did she see, when did she return to Louisville? As she answers, Wilson takes notes. Then Emmert says, "You were in Louisville all day Saturday until you drove to Lexington around 10:30 p.m."

"That's correct."

"Where were you between the hours of seven and ten-thirty Saturday evening?"

"At my new business, and here at home."

"Tell me about your new business."

She does. Then he says, "So how long were you there?"

"A couple of hours. Then, around ten, I came to the house and packed for my trip to Lexington."

"You spent a couple of hours at your new business before coming home to pack?"

"Yes sir."

"It's just vacant space, isn't it? What could you possibly do there for two full hours?"

"I took measurements, did some space-planning, checked out the quality of the ceiling tiles, worked out my color schemes. But mostly I daydreamed."

"Excuse me?"

"This is a brand new business, Detective. It's a big step for me, and I'm very excited about it. I'd like to tell you I spent the whole afternoon and evening doing all sorts of important business things, but the truth is I was mostly daydreaming about having my own business and getting a feel for how it would look, and what items I'd buy to put on display, and stuff like that."

"I see. And where did you get the money to fund this venture?"

"My parents."

"How much did they contribute?"

"A hundred percent."

They look at each other. Then Emmert says, "You used *none* of your personal funds?"

Lindy laughs. "I don't have any personal funds."

"Did your parents take out a bank loan?"

"No sir. My dad set up an LLC for me and opened a business checking account at the bank with a $30,000 deposit. He negotiated the lease and the build out for me. He's pretty much done everything."

"Must be nice," Wilson murmurs, as he jots it down in his notebook.

Emmert says, "What can you tell us about Ian Keller?"

"Well, I know him about as well as I knew Claiburn. He's also studying to be an actor."

"Have you ever been to his apartment?"

"A few times."

"Can you tell us the reason for those visits?"

"We were rehearsing a skit for our acting class."

"Just the two of you?"

"No. All four of us were there: me, Ian, Rayburn and Claiburn. The instructor grouped us together and assigned us a skit. We met at Ian's a couple of times to write and rehearse it. After the performance, we met again to critique it."

"I see. And what was the nature of this skit?"

"You mean the plot?"

"Yeah."

"Home invasion."

Wilson drops his pen.

Chapter 35

"CAN YOU EXCUSE us a moment?" Emmert says.

"You want me to leave the room?"

"No. We'll go outside. But just for a couple of minutes, okay?"

"Whatever."

A few minutes later, they're back in the den. Emmert says, "Mind if we record this?"

She frowns. "Is something wrong?"

"No. It's just that we have a lot of questions, and John's a slow writer. It would save us a lot of time if we could record your answers."

"Okay."

She sees the slightest hint of a smile in his lips: a smug one. This, because actors are trained to notice such things. She likes the subtlety of it. It's something she can use, should she ever find herself on stage. She practices it a couple of times, then files it away for future reference.

"Are you okay?" Wilson says.

"Yes. Why do you ask?"

"It seemed like your mouth was twitching. Do you need to get some water or something?"

"No. I'm fine." *Note to self: more subtlety!*

Emmert turns on the recorder, announces the time, place, and who's in the room. He says they're investigating the death of Claiburn Foster, of Louisville, Kentucky, and asks Lindy to state her name, address, and date of birth. Then he says "We've arrested Ian Keller and Rayburn Foster in connection with the death and possible murder of Claiburn Foster that took place in the South parking lot of the Devonshire Hotel on the twenty-fourth of September, 2016, at approximately nine-twenty p.m."

Then he says, "Lindy, you should be aware that Ian Keller and Rayburn Foster have fingered you—"

"*Whaaat?*" Lindy says, jumping to her feet.

"Jesus, Steve!" Wilson says.

"What's wrong?"

"They *fingered* her?"

"Well, yeah. I mean, they named her as..." It hits him. "Oh. Shit." He shakes his head. "Sorry, Ms. Bissel." He looks at Wilson, who says, "Rewind the tape, Steve. We need to start over."

They do, and this time Emmert chooses his words more carefully: "You may have seen news reports that Keller and Foster have confessed to murdering Foster's brother, Claiburn. They also confessed to committing a string of armed robberies that netted hundreds of thousands of dollars in stolen goods."

"So I've heard. But how does that involve me?"

"They named you as a co-conspirator."

"To what?"

"The armed robberies."

"Wait: they're saying I *robbed* people? With a *gun?*"

He looks her in the eyes. "Actually, they claim you're the mastermind."

She laughs.

"They've given us names, dates, and supporting facts. If you don't mind, we'd like to ask you about those."

Lindy says, "Let me guess: you guys went outside and thought, 'Lindy just admitted she and the guys were practicing an armed robbery script. Maybe we should take her downtown and question her.' But then you thought, 'uh oh, by then she'll have an attorney. Right now she's alone, and she *trusts* us, so let's get what we can before Mom comes home and demands an attorney.' Is that about right?"

"No. We simply thought we could save time by getting your responses to the allegations. If you'd like an attorney it's within your rights to request one. Is that what you'd like?"

"Not really."

They look at each other, and she waits for it...the little smug smile Emmert showed earlier, but she doesn't see it. He announces: "Are you in fact waiving your right to an attorney?"

"For now," she says, and there it is: the little smile that tells her Emmert thinks he's got her right where he wants her.

But Lindy's covered her tracks. She's enjoying this. It's giving her valuable insights into how police detectives question suspects. If she had demanded an attorney, it wouldn't be the same. This is the real deal. It's raw. It's how they take advantage of people and break their stories down.

But to Lindy, it's exhilarating!

Detective Emmert starts by saying: "Did you organize and participate in the armed robbery of Ryan and Nancy Bissel?"

"My own *parents*?" She laughs out loud.

Wilson frowns. "You find that funny?"

"I find it hilarious. Ian and Rayburn told you I robbed my own parents at gunpoint?"

"How about I ask the questions and you answer them?"

"Fine. But the answer's no. I never robbed my parents. Nor have they ever been robbed." She laughs again. "Unless you're counting my private school and college education."

"We fully intend to ask your parents the same question."

"Go ahead. But don't tell them what I said about the costs of my education. That's a sore subject."

"Where did you attend college?"

"Indiana University in Bloomington."

"And did you graduate?"

"Yes sir."

"Excuse me?"

"I graduated last semester."

He frowns. "You didn't fail your last semester?"

"Nope. Just the opposite."

"What do you mean?"

"I could have graduated a semester early. I actually took more classes than required. I wanted to make the most of my education."

"If we contact the Bursar's office at IU they'll corroborate you've earned a diploma?"

"I certainly hope so! I graduated with honors."

"If it's not true, you should tell us now, because we're going to check."

"I have no problem with you checking. If you'd like, I'll show you my diploma."

"You have it?"

"It's in my room. Want me to get it?"

He looks at Detective Wilson.

Wilson says, "Why not?"

She leaves the room, returns a minute later with her diploma and hands it to Emmert. He reads it carefully, then takes a picture of it with his cell phone, and hands it to Wilson. After scanning it a few seconds, Wilson hands it back and she places it on the coffee table.

Then Emmert says: "Tell us about your sorority."

Lindy says, "What sorority?"

Chapter 36

"THE SORORITY YOU were president of," Emmert says.

"I have no idea what you're talking about. I've never been *in* a sorority, much less president of one."

The detectives look stunned. Emmert says, "You certainly *look* like a sorority girl."

"In what way?"

"You're rich, beautiful, smart, you dress well..."

"Thanks. I think. Sorry detectives, but I was a total nerd in college. You know the type: honor society, social justice, sustainable efforts, young professionals, student ambassador...that multiple."

"But you wanted to be an actress?"

For a moment she looks confused. Then she says, "Right. Because I took acting classes. Actually, no. Like I said, I'm a nerd. I'm not a gregarious person by nature. I took acting classes to improve my social interaction skills."

"Tell us about Jenny Reinhold."

"I have no idea who that is."

"She went to IU."

"When?"

"She's still there. She's a senior."

"Well, there are what, 20,000 coeds enrolled there? What makes her unique?"

"She and her family were robbed by Keller and the Foster brothers last Friday night."

"Where?"

"In their home."

"Here in town?"

"Nashville area. We're going to speak to her later today. When we ask if she knows you, what do you think she'll say?"

"I think she'll say no."

"And you can't recall having seen her?"

"No. Sorry."

"She nearly died."

Lindy looks shocked. "When?"

"Friday night. Ian Keller fractured her skull."

"That's *terrible!*"

"Isn't it?"

They're quiet till Wilson says, "Tell us about Terri Wilcox."

"That one I know."

"You do?"

"I saw her everywhere in college." She laughs. "*She's* the sorority girl."

"Were you friends?"

"I'm not sure we ever met. She wouldn't know me, but everyone knows Terri Wilcox. She was super popular." Lindy pauses. "Was *she* part of the gang?"

Wilson gives her a curious look. "Why would you say that?"

Lindy shrugs. "I don't know. She's smart, athletic, pretty. Girls loved her, guys loved her. She'd have a ton of contacts. In fact..." her voice trails off.

"What were you about to say?"

"I think she was pretty high up in one of the sororities. Like president, or rush chairman, or something."

"Is that what you were about to say just now?"

"No. I was going to say she sounds like the person you're making me out to be."

"That's an interesting observation."

"Is it? Why?"

"Because she was brutalized recently."

He studies her face as she absorbs the news.

Lindy says, "You're trying to get a read on my reactions right now."

"I can't speak for Detective Emmert, but my take is you don't seem to care."

"It's not that. It's...you said she was brutalized. I guess I was waiting for you to say something more. It's not enough information. I mean, Terri and I weren't friends. I noticed her at various events because she stood out. But I've told everything I know about her."

"Even so, I would have expected a bigger reaction from you."

"Like I said, I'm a nerd. I tend to analyze data before reacting. 'Brutalized' sounds horrible. But two nights ago Rayburn Foster was beaten to death, and a moment ago you said another girl had her skull fractured and was nearly killed. I guess I was thinking whatever happened to Terri wasn't as serious." She pauses. "Was it?"

"It was serious enough."

Emmert says, "Ever spend the night at Terri's house?"

"She has a *house* already?"

"I'm speaking of her parents' home."

"Are you kidding? I don't even know what *state* they live in."

The detectives look at each other. Emmert says, "Anything else you can think of?"

Wilson shakes his head. Then says, "Thanks for your time. I guess we're done...for now."

As they stand to leave, they hear a beep. Lindy says, "Mom's home. Want to meet her?"

Emmert smiles. "We'd love to!"

Chapter 37

AFTER INTRODUCING HER mom to the detectives, Lindy says, "These guys have been grilling me without an attorney present for a half hour. They think I've been masterminding a gang of armed robbers who break into homes and brutalize women."

Detective Emmert's eyes pop out of his head. "Ma'am, that's—"

Nancy Bissel waves him off with a laugh. "You don't need to defend yourself, Detective. My daughter can be quite the smart aleck when she's with people she likes. Though I must say it makes me nervous to know she's comfortable with homicide detectives. Is this about that poor boy in Lindy's acting class?"

"Yes ma'am."

"Well, I'm sure Lindy would be happy to cooperate any way she can."

"Actually, she's been very cooperative. Mind if we ask *you* a few questions?"

"Well..."

"Just to corroborate a few background points Lindy supplied."

"Such as?"

"Where did Lindy attend college?"

"Indiana University."

"And how many credits does she need to graduate?"

"None. I mean, she graduated last May. Derby Day, actually."

"Derby Day?"

"Yes. First Saturday in May. Can you believe it? Holding a graduation service on Derby Day?" She laughs. "Of course, the school's in Bloomington, not Louisville, or they'd know better. Still, we had to give up our tickets. We gave them to the Robinsons. Do you know them? Bob and Claire Robinson?"

"Mom," Lindy says.

"No ma'am, I'm afraid we don't. Can you tell us the name of Lindy's sorority?"

"Sorority?"

"The one she was president of."

Nancy laughs. "Lindy has many strengths, but I'm afraid being social isn't one of them. She's more of a loner." She looks at her daughter and smiles. "But she's brilliant, and beautiful, and so incredibly wonderful! I wouldn't trade her for the world."

Lindy rolls her eyes.

Detective Wilson says, "Mrs. Bissel, were you and your husband robbed in a home invasion recently?"

"*What?*"

"It's okay to tell the truth. We've captured the perpetrators. Your family's 100% safe. That's really why we're here: to let you know we've caught the men who did it, and to reassure you they're going to prison for many years."

"There's obviously a mistake. We weren't robbed."

He checks his notes. "This would have been the night of September second. A Friday."

Nancy laughs. "You don't need to give me dates. I'd remember if we were robbed."

"And you weren't?"

"Of *course* not! If we *had* been we certainly would have called the police."

"Would you be willing to take a polygraph test?"

"Are you serious?"

"I am."

"Is that really necessary?"

"It would be helpful."

"Well, I suppose so. Can my husband come with me?"

"That would be great. We'd like to hook him up too."

"I can't speak for Ryan, but he might not mind. If I can talk him into coming. Where would this take place?"

"Police headquarters, downtown. We could meet you at 8:00 a.m."

Nancy nods. "Very well. But I must say, it seems crazy to me. I mean, do people really lie about being *robbed*?"

"They do if they're frightened enough. Does that make sense?"

"Not really. It seems to me if they lied because they were frightened they wouldn't *want* to take a lie detector test. It would prove they were lying about the thing they were too frightened to admit the first time around."

Lindy laughs. "You could have said it better, Mom, but you definitely made sense. The reason they want you to take a lie detector test is because the men who killed Claiburn are saying *I* was involved."

"*You?*"

"Yup. What I said earlier is true: Ian Keller and Rayburn Foster told the detectives I masterminded a series of robberies, and said you and Dad were two of the victims."

"That's ridiculous!"

Emmert says, "Mrs. Bissel, it's our job to *investigate* the allegations, not to *believe* them."

"Well, thank you for saying that. Because how could *anyone* believe Lindy's capable of illegal behavior? Nor would she have the *time*! She's been planning this reselling business for more than a year. She even wrote a paper on it for her business class. Has she told you about it?"

"Bits and pieces. I understand you and your husband financed it?"

"Ryan did. Can you excuse me a minute? I'll be right back."

Nancy leaves the room.

The detectives look at Lindy like *What the fuck?*

She laughs. "What can I say? *You're* the ones who wanted to meet her."

Moments later Nancy returns, saying, "Lindy's totally dedicated to her new business. She's been working on it night and day." She holds up Lindy's blue notebook. "You should see her: she's constantly writing down her plans and goals."

Without skipping a beat, Emmert reaches his hand out and says, "May I?"

Lindy says, "No! It's private, actually."

"Oh, don't be silly, honey!" her mom says. "I want the detectives to see exactly what you've been up to."

"Mom? *Stop!*"

Chapter 38

LINDY TRIES TO intercept the handoff, but Wilson gets there first. He accepts the notebook, looks at the cover, and reads: "*Every Last Dime*. Interesting title. How does it relate to your reselling business?"

Lindy sits on the couch and says nothing.

Nancy says, "It's the name of her store: *Every Last Dime*. Get it?"

"No ma'am."

"It's so clever! The customers bring their items, like bicycles and prom dresses as so forth, and Lindy helps them get every last dime of value from them. Don't you just *love* it?"

"I do. Mind if I sit a minute while glancing through it?"

"Please. Make yourself at home. Would you like some coffee or tea?"

"Coffee sounds great."

"Lindy?" Nancy says. "Can I get you something?"

"No thanks. Really, you've done enough."

Emmert laughs. When Nancy leaves the room he winks and says, "You just never know. Before your mom showed up, I was 100% convinced you were innocent. And now look where we are."

"Where's that?" Lindy says.

He looks at Wilson, then her. "According to Keller and Foster, *Every Last Dime* is what you planned to get from your victims."

"And you're saying what, exactly?"

"According to them, your blue notebook of the same name contains the list of past, present, and future victims."

"I see. And so my parents should be in there? And that Jenny girl who nearly died? And Terri Wilcox?"

"That's my guess."

"Well, I hate to break it to you, but—"

Detective Wilson closes the book, looks at Emmert. "Dead end."

"What do you mean?"

"It's all about the business."

"Let me see."

Emmert studies the names and phone numbers: there's a leasing agent, a contractor, a roofer, a plumber, an air conditioning guy, a sign company, and various others. There are a series of dates when specific things need to be done, such as installing the phone service, Internet, electrical, gas, water, trash, and so forth. There's a page dedicated to carpet and tile stores and descriptions of various carpets, and the prices of each. Same with the tile she needs. There are pages of store measurements, lease notes, and a detailed business plan. There's a page for all her banking information, including her loan manager, terms of the note, and so forth.

Nancy's right: her daughter's been very busy. But not busy robbing people. Wilson just has one question for Lindy: "Why didn't you want us to see this?"

"It's an invasion of privacy."

"How so?"

"They're my scattered notes. It's a work in progress. There are probably mistakes. It's like if you're a writer, and someone told me you've been cheating on your wife, and I walk in off the street, grab your unfinished manuscript and start reading. It doesn't matter if there's no proof you cheated on your wife. You'd still consider it an invasion of your privacy."

"I get that. I'm sorry."

"It's okay."

Nancy comes in with the coffee. They have a few sips, then Wilson asks: "Can I get your date of birth?"

She tells him.

"And your husband's?"

She tells him.

Do you off-hand know your social security number?"

"Yes."

"Can I have it for background?"

"Is it safe to share that?"

"With the general public? No. But we're police detectives, and you'd be saving me a call. I can get it from your driver's records if necessary, but it's one more hassle."

She shrugs and gives him her social security number.

"Do you know your husband's?"

"Just the last four digits." She tells him, and he writes it down.

"Emmert says, "By any chance, does Lindy have an apartment in Dallas?"

"Dallas? Were you not paying attention? Lindy's opening a business here in town. She just signed a five-year lease."

"Yes ma'am. I understand. I just wanted to be certain."

They exchange a few minutes of small talk, then the detectives thank Nancy for the coffee, and leave.

"That was odd," Nancy says.

Lindy nods, goes straight to her bathroom, closes the door, and practices making the smug little smile Detective Emmert taught her.

Chapter 39

"GUESS HOW MANY of your claims matched up, Ian?"

"All of them?"

"None of them," Emmert says.

Keller smirks. "You're trying to trick me."

"Keep telling yourself that. In the meantime, here's a quick recap: you said Lindy Bissel was the president of a sorority at IU. She was never in a sorority. You said she failed out of college. She graduated with honors. You said she had an apartment in Dallas but was afraid to move there. There is no such apartment. You said she came up with the plan to start a reselling business last week. Didn't it seem strange to you she already had the keys to a space ready to be built out?"

"She's good at making things happen."

"Especially after planning it for a year. You said she financed the store with her own money?"

"That's right."

"We talked to the loan officer at the bank. He confirmed her father put up the entire thirty grand months ago when they set up her Limited Liability Company called—are you ready for this? — *Every Last Dime*. To put the cherry on top, her neon sign has already been made."

"That's bullshit."

"Is it? Well, hold onto your seat, because there's more: you said Lindy set her own parents up to be robbed so your gang could have a practice run?"

"That's right. And I was there!"

"Well, someone needs to tell her mom, 'cause Nancy certainly knows nothing about it."

"She's afraid to tell the truth. Afraid we'll hurt Lindy."

"She didn't appear the least bit afraid to me and Detective Wilson a couple hours ago. As a matter of fact, she and her husband are coming to the station tomorrow to take a lie detector test."

"Bullshit!"

"You keep saying that, but I'm not sure it's relevant for anything beyond your accusations. Speaking of which, you remember giving us a voice recording of Nancy and Ryan Bissel giving you their social security numbers and dates of birth during their alleged robbery?"

"Of course. So what?"

"They don't match."

He frowns. "They obviously lied to me during the robbery."

"How do you explain the fact that in real life Nancy's voice sounds nothing like the woman on your recording?"

"She must have disguised her voice."

"Today, or during the robbery?"

"How would *I* know?"

Emmert laughs. "You know what Detective Wilson and I think? We think you gave us one of your acting class recordings."

Keller says nothing.

"Let's talk about the blue notebook you told us about. The one titled *Every Last Dime*."

"What about it?"

"We found it. And read it. And every word has to do with her business."

Keller shakes his head. "That's bullshit."

"So you keep saying."

"What about the hotel? Did you check with the front desk?"

"Yeah. She wasn't registered."

"She probably used a fake name."

"Of course she did," he says, sarcastically. "Why wouldn't she?"

"Did you check the sheets for DNA and take fingerprints and stuff like that?"

"Fingerprints in a hotel room mean nothing. They could be a month old if the cleaning crew sucks."

"But the sheets would prove she and Claiburn had sex."

"Yes they would. And if their DNA comes back it would absolutely make her a liar. But it wouldn't prove she masterminded a series of home invasions."

"But if you can prove she lied about *that*, wouldn't it make you wonder if she lied about everything else?"

"Not necessarily, because everyone lies about sex. And frankly, Lindy Bissel is brilliant, and Claiburn was dull, intellectually. And looks-wise, they weren't in the same species."

"Opposites attract."

"I'd bet serious coin they weren't having sex. But if they *were*, I can see why she wouldn't want people to know."

"Were you able to get the sheets?"

"Yeah. And the spread and pillow cases. Not surprising, since you were thoughtful enough to kill Claiburn in the hotel parking lot, which allowed us to evacuate all the guests from the property and shut the hotel down for two days. No one in, no one out. So yeah, we got the sheets. But it'll take weeks to get the DNA results. And like I said, it won't be enough to convict her. And if we don't convict her, your plea deal goes out the window."

"How can I help?"

"I'm not sure you can, Ian. Either you've lied to us twenty times, or she's the best I ever encountered."

"If you thought I was lying, we wouldn't be talking right now."

"Not true. It just means I'm thorough. But you're right about one thing: Detective Wilson and I have doubts about Lindy, but only because she had a perfect answer for everything. Even innocent people can't explain *everything*."

"Have you talked to the other families? The ones we robbed?"

"We'll do that tomorrow after our 8:30 appointment. Detective Wilson's heading to Nashville, and I'm meeting Terri Wilcox and her parents in Indianapolis."

Keller grins. "Good. *That'll* prove me right!"

"Don't be too sure about that. Ever heard of UTK?"

Keller shakes his head.

"University of Tennessee at Knoxville. They offer a degree in Retail, Hospitality, and Tourism Management."

"So?"

"That's why Jenny Reinhold chose UTK. She's been going there for three years. She's never stepped foot on the IU campus."

"Maybe she's in a sister sorority."

"She's not in a sorority at all. Want me to drive another nail in your coffin?"

Ian shrugs.

Emmett says: "She's never heard of Lindy Bissel."

"Bullshit!"

"Your favorite word."

"Maybe Lindy's using an alias."

"Right. Cling to that hope and see where it gets you."

"If they don't know each other, how did Lindy get all that information about her?"

"Good question. But the simplest answer is she didn't, and you're trying to frame her. But either way, let's be clear about something: the fact that I'm checking out your story doesn't mean I'm on your side. I'm not. In fact, I'm going to do everything I can to make sure you do maximum time whether Lindy's involved or not."

"What about Terri Wilcox?"

"What about her?"

"I guarantee you she knows Lindy. There's something personal between them. Otherwise, Lindy wouldn't have asked us to hurt her."

"We'll see. I haven't asked her yet." Emmert opens his briefcase, removes a photo, slides it across the table. Tell me about this lady."

Keller stares at the woman's face. "What about her?"

"Who is she?"

"How should I know?"

"Look again. Be certain."

He takes another look. "I have no clue."

Emmert takes a moment to glance at the two-way mirror where Detective Wilson is standing, recording the discussion. Then Emmert removes another photo from his briefcase and says, "Ever see this guy?"

"Nope."

"Again, Ian. Take your time. Be certain."

"I don't know what you're trying to pin on me, but I don't know these people."

"You're saying you've never seen them before?"

"That's what I'm saying. Who the fuck are they?"

"Nancy and Ryan Bissel: Lindy's parents."

"Bullshit!"

Chapter 40

"SHE LOOKS VAGUELY familiar," Terri Wilcox says, after staring at Lindy's photo a long time. "But I don't know her. She's definitely not a sorority girl."

"Are you sure?" Emmert says. "I'm told there are 3,000 young women in sororities at IU. You couldn't possibly know them all."

"I wouldn't know them all *personally*, but most of us went to the same parties and events. Also, there are only a couple of hot spots in Bloomington. This girl is gorgeous. If she's my age, we would have bumped into each other dozens of times during our four years. I definitely would have remembered her."

"Is it possible she attended IU and never went to any of the events or hotspots?"

Terri laughs. "She'd have to be the biggest nerd on campus."

"So she's never spent the weekend in your home?"

Terri gives him a look. With great condescension, she says, "If this girl spent the weekend in *your* home, do you think *you'd* remember?"

He laughs. "I would indeed."

He looks at Joe and Kim Wilcox. They shake their heads. They don't recognize her either.

"Any additional details you can tell us about the robbery?"

Joe grits his teeth. Kim shakes her head. They're furious. Barely holding it in.

"Well, if you think of anything, please don't hesitate to call."

Emmert doubted he'd hear from them again. While $150,000 is a lot of money, it's apparently not Joe Wilcox money. This he deduced after witnessing Joe and Kim's non-reaction to the news that Louisville police recovered half the gold and silver coins and a possible lead on Kim's stolen bracelet. Nor did Joe seem particularly relieved the robbers were in custody and one was dead. Could it be he planned to hire someone to track them down and punish them personally for what they did to Terri?

One part of Keller's story checks out: he said Terri and Ethan didn't know about the robbery, and they clearly didn't. So there's that. Emmert understands why Joe and Kim never told the kids they were robbed at gunpoint, but he was surprised that three days later, when Terri was assaulted outside the bar, they *still* refused to come forward. Nor had they cooperated today after finally admitting their home had been invaded. All they gave Emmert was: "Three men wearing ski masks."

"How many spoke?"

"One."

"What type of guns did they have?"

"Automatic rifles."

"How tall were they?"

"Average."

"All three?"

"About the same."

"Weight?"

"About the same."

"Anything unusual about the man's voice?"

"No."

"Would you recognize it if you heard it again?"

"*I* would," Terri said.

"Good. We'll need you to testify at their trial."

"No problem. I hope they burn in hell."

Minutes later, in his police sedan, it strikes Emmert that Joe and Kim never bothered to ask when they could get their coins back. *I don't care how rich you are*, he thought. *You'd ask about your money, wouldn't you?*

Emmert certainly would.

He checks his list. Of the 38 twenty-four-hour pawn shops in Indianapolis, only four are located within a mile of the spot where Ian claims he dumped Kim Wilcox's bracelet. And only one is within 100 feet. He checks the photo he took of Kim's ring: the $20,000 one that perfectly matches the 18kt white gold Bulgari bracelet Ian and the twins stole. According to the company, the bracelet retails for $90,000 but is currently on sale for $76,500. "Quite the bargain!" the salesman insisted over the phone.

Emmert calls Mimi Johnson—his contact at the Indianapolis PD—and tells her the Wilcoxes admitted they'd been robbed. He shares the details on the stolen bracelet, and texts her the photo of the matching ring.

"We'll want to interview the Wilcoxes," Mimi says.

"Of course. But can you try to recover the bracelet first?"

Emmert texts her the addresses of the four 24-hour pawn shops.

"Why the all-nighters?" Mimi asks.

"According to Ian Keller, he dumped the bracelet at night. If you found it after dark you'd try to pawn it immediately, wouldn't you?"

"Is that what you think of me?" she said. "That I'd try to cash in on a stolen bracelet?"

"What? No! I mean, I wasn't—"

She laughs so loudly it nearly hurts his ears. It's a full-bodied laugh, the kind that makes him feel silly and lonely at the same time. Though he knows nothing about Mimi, it's a safe bet her laughter would improve the dynamic of his quiet apartment and empty life.

When at last she falls silent he bites his lip and wills himself to ask: "Would you consider getting together, maybe share some ideas?"

"Why?"

"It's a little odd that Joe and Kim never asked about getting their gold and silver coins back, don't you think?"

"Are you asking me out?"

"No."

She laughs.

He says, "I mean...if I *did*, would you consider it?"

"I'll admit you sound pleasant," she says. "But you're coming across kind of needy. The truth is, I don't know a thing about you."

"Well, I'm a nice guy, I'm fun, I feel like we've built a good rapport, and—"

"Whoa, Detective. We've spoken exactly once on the phone: this morning. You've never seen me, you know nothing about me. If some other woman had taken this call, would you be asking *her* out?"

"No."

"Then why me?"

"I like your laugh."

She pauses a moment. "How long you been single?"

"About a year."

"It's a tough job. Hard on a marriage."

"How about you? Are you married?"

"No."

Sitting in his car, in the Wilcox's driveway, Emmert does a silent cheer.

"Are you a black man?" Mimi asks.

"*What?* No. Do I *sound* black?"

"No. But neither do I. Some cops won't date a black woman."

"Why not?"

She laughs again. Then says, "You don't have a clue, do you?"

"About what?"

"What you're getting yourself into."

Emmert smiles. "Does that mean you'll go out with me?"

"No. But it *does* mean I'll meet you for a drink. We'll look each other over, decide how damaged the other one is, then make our decisions. How's *that* sound?"

"Perfect."

"Can I ask you a favor, Steve?"

"Of course."

"When you meet me, don't freak out."

"What do you mean?"

"I'm awfully cute."

He laughs.

"Want to come to the station or meet in a coffee shop?"

"Coffee shop."

"Good answer. Can you give me an hour?"

"Damn!"

"What's wrong?"

"I've only got 59 minutes to give."

It was a stupid remark, but he hoped it might make her laugh. Instead, she asked, "What do you mean?"

"Sorry, I was trying to be funny."

"Don't give up your day job, Detective."

Before hanging up she names the coffee shop and he locates the address on Google Maps and punches it in his phone. He pulls out of the driveway with a hopeful heart, completely oblivious to the war raging behind him inside the Wilcox home where Terri's screaming: "How could you not tell us there was an armed robbery going on in the house while we were in it? If you'd told me, I would've been more careful, and those bastards wouldn't have raped me."

"They didn't *rape* you," her brother Ethan says. They shoved a can of pepper spray up your ass."

She slaps his face and yells, "Shut up you fucking little bastard!"

Kim yelling at Terri: "Don't you *dare* hit him. Maybe if you didn't wear skin tight yoga pants you wouldn't attract so much attention."

"It didn't matter what I was wearing. I could have worn a suit of armor and they still would have attacked me. Those bastards were *following* me! You could have prevented it." She suddenly starts crying and says, "It's your job to protect us. And you didn't."

"How could we possibly know you'd go to that sort of bar in the first place? It's a well-known drug hangout. Are you taking *drugs?*"

"Yeah. That's it. I'm taking drugs. *Jesus!*"

She stomps out of the room and Kim turns her anger on Joe, who completely ignores her. He's fuming, staring out the window, saying nothing.

When Emmert finally drives away, he tells Kim he's going to his office to review their insurance policy.

"Why?"

"I need to check how much I insured the bracelet and coins for."

"Right *now?*" she says. "You need to do that *now?*"

"No, but it's a good excuse to get the fuck out of this house for 30 minutes. I can't stand the constant screaming."

"Fine. Leave me here like always. It's what you do. Go have fun at your precious office."

He grabs his keys and storms out the door. He's going to the office all right, but not to check his insurance papers. He's going there because that's where his throwaway phone is. The one his married girlfriend gave him so they could exchange phone calls and messages without their spouses finding out about their affair.

It takes him twenty minutes to get there, and of course the office is crowded, so he grabs the phone, gets in his car, and dials her number. It rings six times before the pre-recorded message asks if he wants to leave a message.

He says: "Call me the minute you get this. Any time before 5 o'clock today. It's important."

Then he sits and waits for a call that doesn't come.

After twenty minutes he thinks to check for text messages and finds one from yesterday: *Joe: I need to talk to you. It's urgent.* And there was this: *New phone number.*

He dials it. When she answers he tries to keep his anger in check, saying, "You needed to tell me something?"

"Yes. Thanks for calling me."

"No problem. But before you say anything, who the fuck *are* you?"

He hears her take a deep breath. Then she says, "My real name's Lindy Bissel."

Chapter 41

"SO I'M TOLD," Joe says. "You've got some major explaining to do."

"I agree. When can me meet?"

"Let's start with right now. On the phone."

"Are the police listening in?"

"No."

"Are you recording me?"

"I should have thought to, but I was too pissed to think about it. Should I call back?"

She gives a small laugh. "No, that's okay. Is there anything you'd like to ask before I give you my speech?"

"Yeah. You're twenty-two?"

"Yes."

"So you lied."

"Yes."

"And you were a student at IU?"

"Yes."

"Another lie."

"Why?"

"Are you asking why I lied?"

He says nothing, so she says, "I didn't intend to, but one of the first things you said to me was you had a daughter going to IU. You said she was about to start her senior semester, and you asked if was a student. Like Terri, I was also practically 21, going to IU, but I couldn't let you know that."

"Why not?"

"I didn't want to put ideas in your head."

"Like what?"

"Like, did I know Terri? Was I one of her friends? Would I tell her about our affair? And I certainly didn't want you to think about her when you were with me."

"Bad for business?"

"Originally, yes. But as we got to know each other—"

He interrupts: "Are you married, or was that a lie?"

"That was also a lie. Again, by telling you I was married, and my husband was unemployed, I knew you wouldn't associate me with Terri."

His voice gets quiet. "Did you know her at school?"

"No. I knew who she was, but once I made the connection, I kept my distance. I'm certain she has no idea who I am. Anything else?"

"Two things."

She waits.

He says, "I feel like such an idiot."

"Please don't. I have true feelings for you, Joe. Ask your questions. I'll tell you everything."

"I'm going to go out on a limb and assume you lied about my being your first and only customer."

"That was the truth. Surely you could tell how nervous I was that first time."

"I thought so then, but an hour ago a police detective came to my house and told me you're an actress."

"Oh please. I took a stupid acting class this summer, a full year after meeting you. And I only did it to help me deal with the public. I've *seen* you since then. I've *told* you this."

"Yes you did. But you told me a lot of things. Mostly lies."

"That's unfair."

"Is it? Well how about we come to my big question? Then we'll see how unfair I'm being."

"Fine."

"What part did you play in robbing me and Kim at gunpoint?"

"None. I mean, not directly."

"What's that supposed to mean?"

"I'll explain after you ask me the real question: you want to know if I had anything to do with assaulting Terri, and if so, why, and how could I possibly do that to you."

"That's right. So what's your answer?"

"The answer is no. I had no idea. But...can we meet somewhere? I'd like to tell you this in person."

"Sorry. I need to know right now. And you're more than two hours away, so unless you sprouted wings—"

"Joe? I'm here."

"What?"

"I'm watching you right now."

"What the *fuck?*" He looks up. Doesn't see her. Whirls around in his seat. Sees nothing. "You're *here?*"

"Yes."

"*Where?*"

"Gray car, in the far corner."

"You came to my *office?*"

"I followed you here from your house."

"Why?"

"I called you yesterday to warn you about Detective Emmert, and to explain everything that's happened. But you didn't get my message, so you were left hanging. I came because I wanted to tell you my side of the story. And also because I wanted to see you again. It's been six weeks."

"This is crazy. You're stalking me! This is fucked up, Janie."

"Lindy. And it's not crazy. I care about you, Joe. I wanted to set the record straight."

"The only thing you wanted to do was keep from getting caught."

She sighs. "Look. I cared enough to rent a car, drive all the way up here and wait for two fucking hours to tell you my side of the story. If you don't want to hear it, I'll drive home."

"You have no idea how it felt to sit there after being robbed in my own home, after my daughter was beaten and sexually assaulted, only to see your photo on my kitchen table as the detective asked my wife and daughter if they knew you. Then I had to hear how you were the same age as Terri, and a student at IU, and that you'd been accused of planning and orchestrating our robbery and Terri's assault."

"You're right. I can't possibly know what that's like. But I knew it was gonna be awful, and that's why I called. I knew you deserved an explanation, and I'm trying to give it."

"I expect your explanation will be nothing but lies."

"That's not fair, Joe. The only lies I've ever told you were designed to protect our relationship."

"I brought you to my house."

"Yes. And we made love in your bed. And it was wonderful."

"Is that how they knew the layout?"

She sighs.

He says, "Is that how they knew about the safe?"

Instead of answering she says, "I got a room here in town. Crowne Plaza, Union Station. I'm heading there now. If you want to see me, and hear what I've got to say, follow me there. Or come any time before six tonight. If you can't come right now, please call this number, and I'll tell you my room number. Because it's not in my name."

"Of course it's not."

She pauses a beat, then says, "I really hope you'll follow me there."

"Here's a question for *you*," he says with clipped venom: "How screwed will you be when I leave my wife?"

"It won't affect me in the least, unless you plan to see me more often."

"If I leave Kim, you'll have nothing on me. I could tell the police everything."

"Have I ever once threatened you with our affair?"

She waits. "*Have* I?"

"No."

"Then stop insulting me. I would *never* blackmail you, just as I've never pressured you. Unlock your door, please."

"What?"

"I'm standing beside your car. Please open your door."

He clicks the button and she ends the call and climbs in. Then says, "Hi Honey."

Joe says nothing, so she says, "I'm not asking you to cover for me, I just wanted you to know I've been covering for *you*. But that can end right here and now if that's what you want."

"What are you saying?"

"You need to do what's best for you. Leave Kim or stay with her: that's your choice. Tell the police about our affair: again, your choice. But it won't affect me in the least. It's certainly not proof I robbed you or hurt Terri. The one thing everyone agrees on is I wasn't even there."

"Neither was Charles Manson, when his friends butchered those movie people. But he masterminded it."

Lindy gives him a look. "I'm gonna disregard that comment because I know you're upset. But think it through before telling the police about our relationship, because it *will* devastate Terri and make a mess out of your divorce. Remember, you not only paid a 20-year-old college student for sex, you also brought her into your home and fucked her in your marital bed. That's going to come out in the depositions. And of course, you'll have to admit you solicited a prostitute."

"I never considered you that."

"No you didn't, and I always appreciated it. But the truth is, you found me on an escort website and offered to pay me for sex. And you did. Twice."

"If we're being honest I paid you every time."

"Yes. But I only *charged* you twice. There's a big difference. And that difference is what's going to infuriate Kim, because it proves our relationship was much more than just sex." She pauses. "Joe, if you're looking for a way to punish me, the best weapon you have is to end things between us, because that would break my heart."

"I trusted you."

"I know. And I've always lived up to that trust. When Detective Emmert said you'd been robbed at gunpoint I nearly fainted. My first thought was 'Oh my God, Joe's got a heart condition! Is he okay?' But I sat there stone-faced and told him I'd never met you, or been to your house. I was frightened, and had no clue what was going on, but I still refused to say anything that could hurt your relationship with your family."

He says nothing.

She says, "This is ridiculous, Joe. We've never had any issues between us. Some of the best times I've ever had were spent with you. And now look at us." She sighs. "Have you thought to ask yourself a simple question?"

"Which one?"

"Why? Why would I rob the only man whose calls I always answer? The one who lifts my spirits, buys me presents, takes me to the finest restaurants, and gives me a thousand dollars every time we're together?"

"They knew about my safe, Lindy."

"*Did* they? Well *I* didn't! Did you ever tell me you had one? Did you ever walk me through your house and say, 'By the way, there's my safe! That's where I keep all my valuables.' Call me stupid, but it never dawned on me to think about it. I was too busy trying to control my emotions. I was thrilled you cared enough about me to show me your home, but terrified Kim or Terri or Ethan might show up unexpectedly."

She shakes her head. "Are you really hung up about the safe? If *you* were a burglar, looking at the outside of your mansion, wouldn't you say 'There's got to be a safe in there somewhere?'"

"I don't know. I'm not a burglar."

"Well...me either. I'm a twenty-two-year-old spoiled brat who's guilty of nothing more than having a monster crush on a man twice my age. This whole *robbery* business? *Jesus*, Joe: I couldn't mastermind a jelly sandwich!"

He smiles in spite of himself.

Lindy says, "I don't know what Detective Emmert told *you*, but yesterday's the first I heard any of this. And what he said was three guys I did four skits with in an acting class accused me of orchestrating a multi-state crime spree. That somehow I—the girl who spent a whole year trying to figure out how to open a fucking *resale* store—taught total strangers...actors with no criminal backgrounds...how to commit armed robberies. And that from start to finish, I accomplished all this in the space of three weeks, using my connections as a sorority girl, which I'm not. And by the way, for our dry run we supposedly robbed my own parents in our home three weeks ago. Well, that was news to me, news to my parents, and even Detective Emmert doesn't believe it."

Lindy gives her words time to sink in. Then says, "Follow me to the hotel. Come to my room. We'll sit down, I'll tell you my story. I promise you'll believe me, because I'm telling the absolute truth. And if you don't, we can call the police together. And while we're waiting for them to show up, you can fuck my brains out."

He thinks about it a minute, then says, "Okay."

Chapter 42

LINDY'S HOTEL ROOM came equipped with a refrigerator stocked with wine and vodka. She offers Joe a drink, but he declines. Then he declines a hug, walks past her, and sits in the chair by the desk. She takes two plastic bottles of water from the fridge, opens one for herself, hands Joe the other, and sits on the side of the bed, facing him.

She says, "I'm not sure what Detective Emmert told you, but it doesn't matter. I'll tell you everything, and if there's something I fail to cover, just ask, and I'll be 100% honest with you."

He says nothing, so she starts in: "A year-and-a-half ago I was about to complete my junior year. It was getting close to summer, and I decided to stay in Bloomington after learning my parents had lined up a waitressing job back in Louisville. They thought that type of work would be character-building, and might help me get over my social awkwardness, but I couldn't stand the idea of interacting with customers, working for minimum wage, splitting tips. I mean, can you just imagine it: 'Hi. I'm Lindy, and I'll be your waitress this evening. Can I get you a beverage?'"

He tries not to chuckle. "There are worse jobs," he says.

"Fine. Be a hard ass. Anyway, for whatever reason, it never fully registered with my parents that the college credit courses I took in high school were applied to my required freshman courses, which meant I was eligible to graduate a full semester early. But I didn't want to."

"Why not?"

"I wasn't ready to face the world. So, just weeks from completing my Junior year, I dropped a course I was acing so my parents wouldn't be notified I was eligible to graduate. Then, two nights before the senior's graduation weekend, I noticed my friend's dad leaving a downtown hotel. I called out to him, but he pretended not to hear me. He walked away at a fast pace, got into his car, and drove away. Seconds later Emily, my roommate, came out of the same hotel lobby, and it hit me like a ton of bricks: Emily was fucking Maggie's dad!"

"How did that make you feel?"

"Confused. So I confronted her, and at first she denied everything. But I kept after her and eventually she broke down and told me she was making a small fortune as a paid escort. Of course I was fascinated how she managed to do that all year without my knowledge, and she began teaching me the on-line escort business. I spent weeks getting my website profile established, and then I paid to link it to various agencies. I was careful to select a stock photo that generally resembled me, but was slightly less attractive, so I'd be a happy surprise to my future clients."

"And then I came along."

"Well yes, but that was later. The minute my profile went live I was inundated with offers. Emily warned me that would happen, because Bloomington's a small town, and everyone in the area wants to bang the newbies. What surprised me was how many men in the general area were into that life."

"So I *wasn't* your first?"

"You were. I was just explaining how I got into the business. But—please don't make a snide remark right now—I didn't want to be a hooker." She pauses, then says, "Okay, so your face says you think that's exactly what I wanted, so...fine. Think what you want. I'm certainly not your first college girl. You fucked *Emily*, after all."

"Not after meeting *you*, I didn't"

She sighs. "I'm not judging. The point is, I wasn't interested in local guys who did it every weekend with a different girl. I wanted to build my business exclusively with visiting dads. I knew there were at least four events each year when dads come to town to see their kids, not counting the basketball games. But it was summer: no dad events, no sports, and so I turned down one request after another—more than a hundred, actually—and then one day in mid-August you clicked on my profile. My website showed that your inquiry came from a computer in Indianapolis, and the weekend you requested was the same week the off-campus students were moving into their houses and apartments. You asked for a late Saturday night, which told me you were probably going to help your son or daughter move into their new place on Saturday, then take him or her out to dinner, and then you'd come back to your hotel room and wait for me to show up at 11:00 p.m."

He says, "Well, you knew all that after a couple of visits, so maybe you're giving yourself too much credit after the fact."

"Maybe so. At any rate, I met you, and you were very patient, and helped get me through that first time. And of course, you were incredibly generous, paid the full $2,000, and when you asked if you could see me the next week I was thrilled. And so we became...would it offend you to say we became a couple?"

"That'll depend on the part of your speech I *don't* know."

"Of course. So anyway, there came a time you invited me to your home. I thought it was a big step. You also talked about how, in a perfect world, you and I might someday live there together."

"But you were married," he says.

"Right. The lie. Well...I was nervous. I had already lied, and things were going really well between us. Plus, I knew you were super infatuated with me, but I also knew you were just daydreaming about a perfect world, and your ideal situation, and so forth. I mean, if you had said, 'Janie—'"

"—Not your real name—"

She frowns. "Nevertheless, if you had said you were going to leave Kim and asked me to leave my pretend husband and move in with you, I would have done it. And I would have confessed to all the lies."

"Tell me about the burglaries and my daughter's assault."

"A few months ago I signed up for a community college acting class. Out of twenty-something people, I got paired up with three guys, and we were assigned various skits. The way it worked, the instructor assigned each group a skit, and we met during the week to work out our parts. A week later, each group gave their ten-minute presentation, and the others would critique the performance. One of our assignments was home invasion robbery, where me and one of the guys were supposed to be the married couple, and the other two were the burglars. After the performance, the guys must have gotten together and decided to try it in real life. So they did."

"And you'd have me believe that these three guys—who don't know me from Adam—drove two hours to my house and robbed us, then came back three nights later and attacked my daughter, Terri. That they chose my house at random. Me, the only guy you ever fucked during your career in the escort business."

"Obviously you weren't chosen by chance. What happened to you was my fault. But I didn't plan it, and had nothing to do with it." She pauses. "So here's the thing: I made the mistake of dating one of the guys. The police don't know it, and I lied to them about it. You're the only one who knows for sure we were dating, apart from the brother, and, I suppose, Ian Keller."

"You were dating the twin. The one they killed."

"That's right. I dated Claiburn a couple of times, but only because I was bored. It certainly wasn't serious. Not on my part, anyway. In other words, we weren't sleeping together. I kissed him a couple of times, but very casually, and beyond that there was no physical contact. But he was smitten, and extremely jealous. When I learned he had jealousy issues, I broke things off. That was shortly after we did the home invasion skit, and it's also the last time I showed up at acting class. But it's also the first time I became aware he was stalking me. What I didn't know was he'd been stalking me since the day I joined the acting class, which means he probably saw me drive to the Brown Hotel to meet you, and he probably saw us having dinner at the English Grill, and he might have known the make and model of your car, and he almost certainly followed me to your home the following weekend. When they decided to do home invasions, I'm sure he chose your house for several reasons: it was out of town, he knew you were wealthy, and he wanted to punish you for being with me."

Joe thinks about it a long time before speaking. Then says, "What about Terri?"

"I have no idea what that was about. I only know Detective Emmert said they attacked her."

"Why would they say you had a personal grudge against her?"

"I don't know. But they also claimed she and I were sorority sisters, and I've never even *pledged* a sorority. They told Emmert I never graduated. They told him they robbed my parents. They said I had an apartment in Dallas. None of those things are true. You said Emmert showed her my photo. Did Terri recognize me?"

"Not really."

"Did she say she'd ever *met* me?"

"No."

"Well, *that* ought to give me some credibility."

"Why would they dump Kim's bracelet?"

"I don't know anything about that. I only know what Detective Emmert told me, and he never mentioned a bracelet. He said there were gold and silver coins, and a couple thousand dollars in cash. Joe, I swear—"

He waves her off, stares at the floor, says nothing. But Lindy notices his face getting redder by the moment. And when he looks up, she sees tears streaming down his face. He tries to speak, but his voice cracks with emotion. He gives up, starts over: "After your friends robbed us I bought Terri a can of pepper spray and showed her how to use it. Like an idiot, she went to some dive bar Sunday night, and for whatever reason, those bastards were waiting for her to come out. When she did, they punched her in the face, dragged her behind her car, pulled her pants down, and *sodomized* her with the pepper spray!"

Lindy shows him a horrified expression, which she slowly morphs into a look of deep concern. She reaches out to him. He resists at first, then tumbles into her arms. They fall to the floor and he cries and she shushes him and tells him it's gonna be okay. She kisses his forehead and cheeks and the side of his head and holds him to her chest, and moments later she lets him do what he likes best, only this time he's doing it harder, and more forcefully, and she winces and takes it, and absorbs every last ounce of pain, because apart from his cheating, and his many weaknesses, Joe's hurting, and it's her fault, and she deserves the punishment. And as he bears down on her she studies his face and tries to memorize each of his changing expressions because that's what great actresses do: they suffer for their craft.

Now, thoroughly spent, he starts whimpering, and Lindy wonders how this fuckwad managed to become a titan of industry. Then she remembers what his father does for a living and it all makes sense. Joe probably couldn't last a day in the real world. This is a guy who started his career on third base and thinks he hit a triple. She comforts him till she reaches her breaking point, then gets to her feet and asks if he's ready for that drink now.

He says, "If I were to leave Kim, once and for all, would you still date me?"

"Do you honestly believe the only reason I'm dating you now is because you're married?"

"No, but—"

"Yes, I'd keep dating you."

"Would you move in with me?"

"Yes. But not right away, since I just signed a five-year lease for my business."

"You could hire someone to run that store and set up a second location here."

"I can't afford a second location."

"I'd help you."

"In that case, I'd move in with you immediately," Lindy says, knowing it will never happen.

"Let me think about it," he says.

"Of course."

"In the meantime, can we keep seeing each other?"

"That's up to you. You've got my number."

Noticing he hasn't thought to pay her yet, she says, "And how could I say no? You've always been so *generous*!"

He instinctively digs into his pocket and starts counting out fifties. When he gets to ten, he places them on the counter, leaving her surprised, curious, and slightly peeved. Is this is his way of punishing her for allowing him to get robbed? Or could it be their new number? If it's the new number, she's just taken a fifty percent pay cut for the second time. This, because their first two fucks cost him two grand each. Then she made him a deal: if he promised to see her exclusively she'd give him a 50% discount. He agreed, and it's been a thousand ever since.

Until now.

And the bottom line, $500 isn't gonna cut it.

Only one thing to do: accept it graciously, with a smile, and give him an excuse next time he calls. And when she finally *does* meet him, she'll deny him the usual oral foreplay. She'll go straight to the fucking, and give him 50% less enthusiasm. He's a smart guy. He'll get the message.

As it turns out, it's not necessary. Her face must have given away her disappointment because he says, "I wasn't expecting to see you, or I would have brought more. This is all I've got, besides some small bills."

She says, "Joe, It's okay. I wasn't frowning about your gift; I was frowning because you're still upset. I had hoped to cheer you up. Was I not attentive enough?" She uses the move she stole from a rerun of *Little House on the Prairie*, where Michael Landon twitches his lips like he's about to cry.

And of course it works.

"Oh my God, yes!" He says. "I'm so sorry! You were wonderful! Here!" He places the rest of his money beside the first stack, including all his pocket change. She rushes over to him and gives him a big hug. "You're so wonderful!" she coos, and means it. Sure, it's the least amount he's ever offered. But he gave her *every last dime*, which she takes as a good omen for her business.

Chapter 43

Five Weeks Later...

THE FRONT ENTRANCE to Lindy's store makes a gentle dinging sound when the door opens. She looks up from her desk to see Detective Emmert, then grins and extends her wrists in case he wants to cuff her.

He laughs.

She says, "Please tell me you brought me something to sell for you."

"Sorry."

She stands and makes a sweeping motion with her hand. "How do you like it?"

"Very impressive."

She starts to say something, but his words come out first: "I'd like to check your inventory."

Lindy laughs. "Still looking for those Krugerrands?"

"As a matter of fact, I am. But you're way too smart to sell them from your store."

"I am? Wow! Flattery will get you everywhere. Unless you seriously think I'm part of the Keller-Foster gang."

"It doesn't matter what I think."

"It matters to me."

He sizes her up. "Well, in that case, no: I don't think you masterminded a series of burglaries using a bunch of incompetent actors. On the other hand, I'm positive you know far more about it than you've admitted."

"For example?"

"For example I can't help but notice this store would be a perfect way to sell stolen goods."

"Even though you said I was too smart to do that."

"I said you were too smart to sell the stolen Krugerrands, should you somehow find yourself in possession of them."

"Not to mention Morgan silver dollars."

"Exactly. But it's easy to imagine criminals flocking here with all sorts of newfound items. They steal them, you store them till they're sold."

"Which is why you want to see my receipts."

"Exactly."

"I'm happy to comply. But I hope you can appreciate I have to take my customer's word that they legally own the goods they give me to sell."

"Of course."

"Being the law-abiding citizen I am, maybe you'll furnish me a list of stolen goods each week so I can keep an eye out for anything suspicious."

"Thanks. I'll probably take you up on that, since I intend to check your inventory every week for the next five years."

She laughs. "My tax dollars at work. So what's the latest on Keller and Foster?"

"It'll probably be a year before they finally go to trial."

"Which of them killed Claiburn?"

"Both. The beating was so frenzied it's impossible to tell who landed the first mortal wound. They'll probably both do twenty years for the murder, plus five more for the assaults and burglaries."

"Did they ever admit they lied about me?"

"No. They're clinging to the story to the bitter end."

"Are they claiming I orchestrated the murder?"

"No, but they hold you responsible. They killed Claiburn because he was going to confess to the police. Supposedly he fell in love with you, but was jealous of the others, and hoped to get immunity by selling them out. That way he'd have you all to himself."

"Well, I hope you know that's absurd."

"I do."

"What are the police saying?"

"As far as my department's concerned, you're out of it."

"But you still plan to check my records each week."

"Just to make sure you're not trafficking in stolen goods."

"Since we're on that subject, which one got Claiburn's money?"

"Neither. They're convinced he gave his share to you at the hotel that night."

"Gosh, I don't recall being at the hotel that night. Did Claiburn book a room there?"

"According to hotel records, he did not. And neither did you."

"Do they think we somehow broke into a hotel room?"

"No. But they claim you were there, and had sex with him, and that was his motivation to go to the police."

"I assume the coroner performed an autopsy."

"He did."

"And can I assume my DNA was nowhere to be found?"

"You can. But you know what else was missing? Claiburn's duffel bag. Rayburn saw him take it into the hotel lobby that night, but he didn't have it when he came out. Also, based on the math, it's clear that each member of the gang got one-fourth of the gold and silver coins."

"Meaning I had the final fourth."

"Plus Claiburn's fourth. That's their story."

"But you don't believe it."

"Let me be clear: I don't believe you were the mastermind. But I *do* believe you were involved."

"Because these guys said so."

"That's right. And because the math says there had to be someone else. If there was anyone else they could name, they would, since it would reduce their sentences by at least two years. But they never wavered. It was you from the start, and it's still you."

She sits on her desktop. "I guess it's a good thing evidence matters. What was the final straw that convinced your department to give up?"

"The DNA evidence."

"Tell me about that."

"Foster and Keller said Claiburn admitted giving you his share of the loot. He also claimed he had sex with you. Obviously, they wanted to prevent him from going to the cops, but they also wanted his share of the loot. But he wouldn't tell them which room you were in, so they beat it out of him."

Lindy arches a brow. "And did they go to the room?"

"No. By then the police showed up."

"I assume they told the cops I was there with the loot."

"They did. And the cops checked with the front desk and found the room was registered to someone else. A couple, who were having dinner off the property, as it turned out. So the cops collected the blanket, sheets, and pillow cases and sent them off to the lab for DNA profiling."

"Which is why you asked me for a saliva sample."

"Right. But the DNA came back negative."

"Were you surprised?"

"Actually, I was. I can't imagine two guys with no prior arrests would beat a friend and brother to death unless a woman was involved."

"But you said it yourself: the DNA evidence showed I wasn't there."

"Yes. But you know what else it showed?"

"What?"

"It showed *Claiburn* wasn't there, either. But we know he was."

"Maybe he went to the hotel to meet someone else and she wouldn't let him in."

"Or maybe Claiburn loved you so much he took a helluva beating before giving them the wrong room number."

They stare at each other until she detects the yearning in his eyes. Then she smiles, and he clears his throat and says, "Let's see those receipts."

"Where would you like to start?"

He points to the showroom items. "We'll start with the least obvious, and work our way through your listings."

"Are you looking for something in particular?"

"Today I just want to make sure the receipts match the inventory. If something looks hinky I'll ask you for names and addresses. If you don't supply them, I'll order a search warrant and confiscate them."

"And next week?"

"We'll do it again. And I'll check the items against a list of stolen property."

"Sounds like a lot of work."

"It's a living."

"You still drink coffee?"

"Like a vampire drinks blood."

"If you tell me your brand I'll make sure you never run dry."

"That's nice of you."

"I'm actually hoping for a favor."

"I'm willing to hear it."

"If you're gonna spend hours here every week my customers might think I'm being investigated. Would you consider working in my back office?"

"I thought that was a bedroom."

"A—*what?*"

He laughs. "Keller and Foster said you were putting a bed in there so you could have sex with them on a regular basis."

Lindy laughs. "Did you at any time believe that?"

"I look at them, I look at you...No. Never." He pauses. "Still..."

"You'd like to take a peek, just the same."

He smiles.

She extends her palm in the direction of the back office. "Make yourself at home."

"What does that mean, exactly?"

"Feel free to snoop."

She hands him her paperwork, he takes it to her office. Thirty minutes later he emerges, saying, "I've gotta give you credit: your records are immaculate."

"Thanks. What's next, the storage shed?"

"Ideally, yes. But you'd have to close your store to show me."

"No problem. I'll leave a note on the door."

Lindy drives to the storage shed, Emmert follows in his sedan. Once there, she walks him through the dozen items, and shows him the paperwork. He pokes around the shed a few more minutes, then thanks her for her time, and drives away.

Now, back at her store, Lindy presses a button on her throwaway phone. When Jackie Keck answers, she says, "I think I'm being followed."

"You're probably just paranoid."

"I agree. But how silly would I feel if I'm right?"

"Want me to find out?"

"Yes."

"When?"

"Closing time."

"Who am I looking for?"

"Black Chevy Caprice. Got a pen?" She checks the photo she took of Emmert's car as he drove away, then gives Jackie his license plate number. "When I close the store tonight, follow me from a distance. I'll drive all over the city. If you see the car, call this number."

"Got it."

Chapter 44

THAT NIGHT LINDY drives 90 minutes, stopping twice along the way. When she finally pulls into her driveway, Jackie calls to say no one followed her.

"Satisfied?" she asks.

"No. If you're available, I'd like you to check as I go to and from work all week. And sometime next week the black sedan will be parked in front of my store. When the guy leaves, I'd like you to follow him and see where he goes."

Lindy ends the call, makes another one. When the guy answers she says, "I've switched phones," and gives him her new number.

He says, "We're still on for tomorrow, right?"

"No. I need to postpone."

"How long?"

"I'm not sure. Probably a week."

"I miss you."

Of course you do. You've probably never had a girl call you before and here I am, talking to you for the sixth time without recoiling in horror. "Thank you, Ronald."

"Do you miss *me?*"

Lindy: holding her breath, looking up at the ceiling of her car, mouthing *Kill me now!*

"*Do you?*" he says.

"Yeah Ronald. I miss you."

"I miss you too."

"Right. So hang tight. I don't have a place or time yet, but I'll be in touch."

"Why can't I ever call *you?*"

"Because those are the *rules*," she snaps. "You *know* this, right?"

"Yeah, but—"

"Act like a professional, Ronald. Okay?"

"You keep calling me Ronald. You know I hate that name."

"You'd like me to call you Ron."

"Yes."

"Sorry, but until you do something great you're Ronald."

She ends the call before he can respond, then thinks, *this guy makes Claiburn look cool!*

Lindy enters her house, gives her eager parents the lowdown on her fourth day on the job: "No sales, but I picked up three customers. Crappy stuff, except for a racing bike I'll be able to turn for two thousand."

"So you'll get...how much from that?" Nancy asks.

"Twenty percent. Four hundred dollars."

"Well, that's a great day!"

"It would be, except the customer wants me to list it for $4,000. And it won't sell for that, so it's gonna sit a while. At some point he'll either accept the $2,000, or he'll take his bike back and I'll get nothing."

"That doesn't seem fair."

"Well, it's the nature of the business."

"You should talk to Dad."

Lindy bites her lip. "Good idea."

She goes to her room, thinking *right. Talk to Dad. Because somehow Dad will know the secret to selling this used, out-of-date racing bike for its original cost.* At least Dad's cool. He won't question her judgement. He trusts her. He's plenty smart, but knows she understands the business better than he does. So yes, she'll talk to Dad. But the only advice she'll ask is "How can I get Mom to back off?"

She dials Henry's number and gives him the same information she gave Ronald: new phone number, delayed meeting, she'll be in touch. This is Lindy, learning from past mistakes: Henry's from Nashville, Ronald's from Cincinnati, and Colin's from Indianapolis. No locals, no brothers, no prior friendships. She found the actors online, lured them with the promise of minor acting jobs, auditioned them in person in their home towns. Since they don't know each other, they're less likely to cheat or turn on her.

Assuming she can coax them into robbing houses.

These aren't the first three guys she contacted. Out of fifteen online videos she personally interviewed seven, and eventually narrowed the field to three physically imposing actor wannabees who were inexperienced with women and skilled enough to learn the dialogue and body language.

She calls Colin and gives him the same spiel.

Colin's the gun guy, but it's mostly hand guns, and he's not as knowledgeable about firearms as the twins had been. Nor does he possess multiple automatic weapons. But he does have one, and it's a doozy: an MP5K sub-machine gun that's smaller than the twins' assault rifles, and even more imposing. Colin calls it the ultimate close-quarters weapon, and when he trotted it out it made her nipples hard for twenty minutes.

Chapter 45

AFTER THREE DAYS without catching sight of the black Caprice, Jackie changed things up by enlisting her husband, Bill, to follow *her*. But after four more days without a sighting, even Lindy had to conclude she wasn't being followed.

It made sense.

Weeks had passed with no further leads, and the police could take credit for busting the gang, solving Claiburn's murder, recovering Kim's bracelet, half the coins, and two-thirds of Melissa Reinhold's missing jewelry. As long as she refused to sell stolen merchandise, Lindy would be fine. If Detective Emmert wants to come in once a week to review her perfect records, no problem. He'll eventually give up and leave her alone.

On the eighth day, Emmert shows up with a three-page list of recently-stolen goods from the general Louisville area. He gives her a copy, she reviews it and says, "You're free to check, but I haven't seen any of these items."

He believes her, but checks her entire inventory anyway.

While he's busy doing that, she contacts Jackie and says: "He's here. Park near the store and wait till he leaves. Then follow him wherever he goes."

That night Jackie calls to say Emmert drove to a fast food restaurant, then downtown to the police station. After a couple of hours, he drove home. "Want his address?"

"I suppose."

Jackie shares it, then says, "Ashley said you called today."

"How's she feeling?"

"About the same."

"Did she tell you I tried to get her to go for a drive?"

"Yes."

"No big deal, just once around the block."

"She's still not ready."

"No, but you wouldn't believe how close she came to saying yes. Next time for sure!"

"I can't tell you what your calls mean to her. And to us. We really appreciate it."

"I'll keep working on her."

"What do you girls talk about for hours at a time?"

"Girl stuff. Mostly I listen, and try to encourage her. But I know for sure she's getting better because just months ago she only wanted to talk about her past."

"Like what?"

"Her best friend from childhood that moved away."

"Jenny Reinhold?"

"I can't remember the girl's name. But now she's talking about the present. I guarantee I'll have her out in the world before you know it."

"She said you've been asking questions about her sorority sisters."

"Actually, I've been collecting names of her former college friends, trying to locate them on social media. Eventually I hope she'll let me contact them to see if they'll call her once in a while, and maybe visit."

"Omigod, Lindy, that's...Wow! I don't know what to say! Thank you!"

"My pleasure. I've always loved Ashley. She was my best friend, freshman year. Until she got in her sorority, anyway. But even afterward, when she became president, she never shunned me, and when she wasn't busy with her friends she always stopped by to visit. She was the only super-popular girl that ever treated me special."

"And now you're returning the favor."

"I'm really just being her friend. Ashley's been through a lot. Don't worry, she'll snap out of this."

"I hope so. By the way, you haven't stopped by to check on your duffel."

Lindy knows this is Jackie, reminding her she hasn't been paid yet this month. "I'm just being careful. I'll stop by later this week."

"Well, everything's just the way you left it. So..."

"Yes?"

"Enough small talk. Got something else for us?"

"I'm working on it."

"Good. Because Bill's out of work and I like my luxuries."

"You always say that."

"It's always true."

"I'll let you know."

Lindy calls her three stooges and sets up a meeting at the Cincinnati Hyatt for the following night. When the guys show up, she sits them at the large table in her suite, introduces them to each other, then starts her spiel:

"Guys, I've seen your work. You're good, solid actors." She hands them each a script and says, "There are two speaking parts. Henry, you'll play the Leader. The entire scene revolves around you. Colin, you're Menace. Your lines are few, but powerful. Ronald, you're Muscle. Your job will be facilitation and body language. The Leader does most of the talking. He's dangerous, but reasonable. Menace is exactly what it implies: his job is to look like he could explode at any moment, and if he does, the bodies will start piling up. And Muscle never speaks. His job is to appear dumb and pervy and drive the getaway car. Now to make it tougher, you'll be wearing these."

She doles out the ski masks.

Colin says, "How are we supposed to emote with masks on?"

"Excellent question. And the answer is eyes and body language."

"What sort of scene is this?" Ronald asks.

"It's called *Home Invasion*."

"Whose home are we supposed to be invading?"

"For now, I'll play the homeowner."

Colin says, "Not to sound mercenary, but I drove two hours to get here tonight."

"I drove five," Henry says.

"My point is—"

Lindy says, "I get your point. I said I'd pay above-scale for rehearsals, and I will. In fact, I'm paying you each $250 for tonight's rehearsal. Don't frown, Henry. That's $250 more than you've made in your entire career as an actor." She catches Ronald sniggering. "You've got nothing to laugh about, Ronald. In fact, none of you has ever been paid a dime for acting. But I'm putting together a troupe. And if you make the cut, you'll be rich in no time."

"Do you have a job lined up?" Colin says.

"Is this like Second City or Saturday Night Live?" Ronald says.

"This is the first rehearsal," Lindy says. "Let's not get ahead of ourselves."

"How many rehearsals are you planning?" Henry says.

"As many as it takes. But you won't have to come all the way to Cincinnati next time. We'll do the next one in Nashville."

"That's five hours for *me!*" Ronald says.

"And me," Henry says.

"That's right. And the third will be Indianapolis. Different home towns make it fair for everyone. Don't forget, I'm driving two to three hours each time as well. But if we need additional rehearsals, we'll do them in Louisville. That said, I expect we'll only need three out-of-town trips before the dry run."

"You mean dress rehearsal?" Ronald says.

"Right. Full wardrobe, ski masks, guns..."

"Real guns?"

"Yes. But no bullets. Say it."

"No bullets."

"Henry? Colin? Say it, please."

They do. Then Lindy says, "Not ever."

"Where will the dress rehearsal take place?" Ronald says.

"Louisville."

"When?"

"When you're ready."

Chapter 46

AFTER REVIEWING THE script for twenty minutes, Henry says, "Something's missing."

Lindy beams. "Tell the others."

"The victims: Mom, Dad, Daughter."

"What about them?" Colin says.

"They don't have any speaking parts after the intro."

Colin and Ronald check the scripts. Ronald says, "Why not?"

"She wants us to go in blind. She set the stage for us, but when the shit goes down she wants to see how we react. She wants us to improvise."

"Exactly," Lindy says. "Because every situation's different. You can plan, but you never know exactly what might happen. Tonight we're assuming the daughter opens the front door, and you guys rush in. But what if someone else opens the door? What if the daughter has a guest spending the night? What if the parents aren't home? What if they don't let you in? What if the mom's upstairs in the tub? Or maybe the dad has a gun hidden under the couch. Generally speaking, what's the first thing you need to do once you've got them rounded up?"

"Check for weapons?"

"That's second. What's first?"

They look at each other.

"Henry?"

"Cuff them?"

"Good. What's third?"

No one knows. She takes her cell phone out of her pocket, presses a button, then plays it on speaker:

What's the first thing you need to do once you've got them rounded up? Check for weapons?

That's second. What's first?

Ronald says, "You're *taping* us?"

Henry sneers. "No, Dipshit. She's showing us number three: we need to confiscate the phones so they can't record us, or call for help."

"That's right," Lindy says. "But we're a team, Henry. And just because it's coming quicker to you at the moment doesn't give you the right to castigate your team members. From now on I want you to act like home invaders. Each of you is critically important to the others, and none of you can do this alone. Henry? I gave you the role of Leader, but that doesn't mean you're in charge of the gang. Now apologize to Ronald."

He frowns.

"You want this role or not?"

"Sorry," he says.

Now shake hands.

"What are we, in third grade?"

"No. But I can't be attracted to any man who disparages his teammates."

He gives her a sly look. "Does that mean you're attracted to me?"

"I'm attracted to *all* of you. And if you like the sound of that you should do all you can to please me. And you do that by working hard, learning your roles, and being good teammates."

"Sorry, Ron," he says. "I was being a jerk."

"No shit you were."

Lindy frowns at him. Ronald takes the cue: "It's all good, Henry."

"Hank."

He nods. "It's all good Hank." They shake hands.

Lindy stands up, walks around the table, gives them each a kiss on the cheek. Then she asks Colin to stand. When he does, she kisses him on the mouth.

"Hey!" Ronald says. "How come he got a real kiss?"

"He didn't say anything bad about his teammates. Don't you think that deserves a reward?"

"*Hell no!*"

Lindy laughs. "In that case, don't kiss him." She pauses. "Now let's get back to this issue about the Leader. Henry's not the leader of this group. It's just the title I gave him because during a home invasion it's best for one person to do the talking. So I named him Leader, but I can just as easily call him Dipshit. Are we clear on this?"

They all nod.

"So who's the leader?"

Ronald says, "No one."

"Wrong. Let me ask it a different way: who's paying you?"

"You are."

"That's right. I'm the leader. This is my screenplay, and my production. Your input counts, but in the end, I make the decisions. If you can live with that, you'll be paid a decent wage during rehearsals, and if all goes according to plan you could literally make a fortune. Can everyone live with that?"

They nod.

She sees Henry marking his script.

"What are you doing?"

"Changing my name to Dipshit."

The guys laugh.

"Please don't," she says. "I was just trying to make an example. I would never disrespect you that way."

"Then call me Hank. No one calls me Henry."

She looks at the others. "Please call him Hank from now on."

They nod.

"What about you?" he says.

"You'll remain Henry until you do something spectacular."

"Like what?"

She smiles. "I'll know it when I see it."

Chapter 47

AFTER THREE HOURS Lindy says, "I can't tell you how impressed I am. How many of you believe you could do a real home invasion right now?"

They all raise their hands.

Hank says, "It's obvious you've done a lot of research. But have you spoken to any actual burglars?"

"Three. And two police detectives, as well."

"The guys you talked to: were they big time?"

"They clipped one homeowner and his wife for more than $150,000 in the space of thirty minutes."

Ronald says, "How'd they get caught?"

"They never did. What happened, there was a fourth person. A mastermind, who put the whole plan together. The mastermind did all the research and planning, picked out all the victims, taught the team members what to do and how to do it. But the team got greedy, felt they were doing all the real work, so they cut the mastermind out."

"How?"

"They only reported half the take and divided the other half three ways instead of four. So the mastermind burned them." She pauses. "There's a lesson here. What is it?"

Henry says, "Never burn the mastermind."

She laughs. "I was looking for never get greedy, but your point's well taken." Lindy rewards him with a kiss on the lips. Then she opens her handbag and removes three checks and hands them to the guys, saying, "It's late, and you've worked really hard. I don't know your schedules, but I'd love for us to get a good night's sleep and hit it again in the morning at eight. Ronald, you're local, so you've already got a place to stay." She points to the interior door. "That's my bedroom, but there's plenty of room in this suite for two rollaway beds. And there's a half-bath. Henry, you and Colin are welcome to crash here tonight."

Colin notices the in-room refrigerator. "What about food?"

"I've paid for the room, but not incidentals, so if you order room service or raid the refrigerator, it's on you."

"Would we be paid another $250 for tomorrow morning?"

"Of course."

"I'm in."

"Me too," Henry says.

"I'll bring donuts," Ronald says.

Outside, in the parking lot, Detective Steve Emmert yawns, checks his watch. Then calls Wilson. "I think she's in for the night."

"Did you get her room number?"

"No, but she's going by Ashley Keck, same name she used to rent the car."

"You should get a room."

"Damn right I should. But you know how this shit works: the minute I do, I'll lose her."

"You're going to sit there all night?"

"Yup."

"Jesus, Steve."

"What can I say? If you'd lost the coin flip you'd be doing the same thing tonight."

"You know I would. But name one other detective who's dumb enough to do it."

Emmert laughs. "They're too busy spending their ill-gotten gains."

Wilson says, "You know what really gets me? All these years we're the ones who never took a dime, never looked the other way. Now they tell us they picked the wrong fund manager twenty years ago and our pensions are practically worthless. You believe that shit?"

"Face it, John: we're saps. Every detective I know is on the take, not to mention half the cops."

"At *least* half the cops. Probably more."

"Plain and simple, we're suckers. Meanwhile, the crooked ones are set for life."

They're quiet till Wilson says, "You ever think about how different our lives would be if we agreed to look the other way once in a while?"

"I think about it every day. Do me a favor?"

"Name it."

"Call me when you get up tomorrow morning. In case I fall asleep."

Chapter 48

IT'S EARLY MORNING, and Lindy and the guys are hitting it hard. Every time they pretend to break into a house, she throws them a different angle. One time she's docile. The next, belligerent. And though she can't scream in the hotel room, she simulates screaming by whispering loudly, same as the guys are doing. Sometimes she plays herself, sometimes one or both parents. But each time it's different, and she's doing all she can to make it as authentic as possible.

That week they do an overnight in Nashville and another in Indianapolis rehearsing the same scenes over and over until the moves and dialogue are second nature. When she's convinced they're at the top of their game, she announces one final meeting to take place at four o'clock the following Friday in Louisville, on the top floor of the airport's short-term parking lot. She tells them to bring their throwaway phones and to use no other phones at any time when talking to her or the other members of the group.

Since Colin's the only one who owns guns, she tells him to bring weapons and wardrobe, but no bullets, and to hide everything in the trunk of his car. The others are to bring wardrobe, which she defines as ski mask, black shirt and pants, sneakers, all of which can be thrown away. She tells them this will be the last meeting before the dress rehearsal, which she's moved to Indianapolis in two weeks, at a location to be determined.

On Friday, when they're all present and accounted for in airport parking, Lindy lines them up beside her rental car and says, "How many of you have broken your promise?" When no one volunteers a response she says: "You promised you wouldn't tell a soul about this project. You agreed not to tell your friends, parents, or loved ones anything about the scenes we've been rehearsing. But you lied. *All* of you."

They break eye contact. Henry and Colin look away. Ronald looks down.

"See?" she says. "This is what separates professionals from wannabees. Professionals know how the system works. They don't buckle under pressure. They have confidence. They don't need to brag. Professionals don't tell their parents or friends things like: 'Okay, I'll tell you, but you can't say a word about this to anyone.' Because professionals know their loved ones can't be trusted because unlike *you* guys, they weren't paid thousands of dollars to *keep their mouths shut!*"

She glares at them like a schoolteacher who caught her best students cheating. "I trusted you. Gave you your big break. Paid you fifteen hundred dollars—the only money you've ever received as actors—with the promise you'd get rich very quickly, and gave you one fucking stipulation: to keep this project 100% confidential. But did you? No!"

No one speaks for a long time. Then Ronald says: "I told my parents. They kept yelling at me, accusing me of wasting my life with the acting classes. They said I was never going to make it, and no one was ever going to give me a role."

"And?"

"In a moment of weakness I..." he sighs. "I fucked up."

"Colin?"

"I told this girl I was going to be in a movie."

"*Be* in a movie? Like an extra?"

"No."

"You told her you had a starring role, did you not?"

"Yeah, but...how did you *know?*"

Lindy didn't. But she knows human nature, and she knows men. "Henry?"

"I told a couple of people. But if you already know that, you know I told them I was rehearsing for a play. A romantic comedy."

"Come here."

When he does, she takes his hand, kisses it, and—as Ronald and Colin's eyes bug out—places it on her breast. "Nice job, Hank." She removes his hand, kisses it again, then kisses his lips. When he gets back in line she says, "I assume the people you told know about the upcoming dress rehearsal in Indianapolis?"

They all nod.

She takes a deep breath. "From here on out, you'll say nothing to anyone, agreed? But if you do find yourself in a bind, do what Hank did: lie your asses off. Do whatever you have to, but don't mention each other's names and don't mention mine. Make up something completely unrelated. Say you're auditioning for a talent agency, or a reality show, or you got a non-speaking role in a car commercial."

They nod again.

"By the way," she says. "I lied, too. The dress rehearsal's not in two weeks, it's tonight. In about—" she checks her phone. "Six hours."

"*What?*" Ronald says. "*Where?*"

"Right here in town. At my parent's house."

Like Keller and the twins that first time, these guys are nervous. Ron's eyes are big as saucers.

"How's it gonna go down?" Colin says, attempting to hide his fear from the others.

"In a few minutes, you guys are gonna get in Ronald's car and follow me. Pay attention to the route so you don't get lost tonight. When we get close to my house I'll call Hank, and he'll put me on speaker. I'll guide you to my parent's house and point it out, but we won't stop. We'll drive past it and go straight to the McDonald's where you're gonna park your car tonight. Then you're gonna hang out, go to a movie, go to dinner, do whatever. At nine forty-five you'll park Ronald's car at McDonald's, change into your wardrobe, with your ski masks tucked into your underwear. When you get to my porch, put the ski masks on and ring the doorbell."

Hank grins. "I might not have enough room in my underwear."

She gives him a look. "Really? Why's that?"

He winks. "I'm pretty big down there."

"Oh yeah? Show me."

"Huh?"

"Pull it out. Show me how big it is."

"What, right *here*?"

Ronald and Colin laugh.

"Yeah right here," she says. "You're the one who's bragging. Be a man: back it up."

His face turns red. Ronald and Colin laugh harder. Lindy says, "C'mon, big shot. Show us how big your dick is. I'm sure we'd all like to see what you consider big."

He feigns cool: "I'll show you later, in private."

"Show me now, or you're Henry again."

He grits his teeth. "Later."

Lindy sighs. "I checked out dozens of actors on the Internet before choosing you guys, and I picked you because I'm physically attracted to you. Every time I watched you playing your parts I envisioned being intimate with you. But now?" She shakes her head. "Maybe I'm wrong. Maybe you have no interest in me sexually, and that's fine. But let me tell you, you're missing out."

Colin says, "I'm interested."

So are the others.

"Good to know," Lindy says. "But if you want to make it happen, you'll have to be more like the guys you play in the script." She sighs again. "I can't tell you how disappointed I am. I was hoping to spend the whole afternoon with you and see what might develop. But then you admitted you broke your promises about keeping things quiet, and now Henry's all puffed up, acting like some sort of porn dude 'cause I let him touch my boob. Grow up guys. We could be such a great group. We could have a ton of fun and make a shitload of money. I'd hate to walk away after all the work we've put in." She pauses. "Is it too much to ask for everyone to be honest and genuine, with no bullshit, no infighting, and no bragging?"

Ronald says, "I've got the world's tiniest dick."

"Whaaat?"

"I guarantee it's the smallest here. It's the size of a toddler's thumb."

Everyone laughs, including Lindy.

Henry says, "Show it."

Ronald unzips his pants, but before he can pull it out Lindy says, "It's okay! I believe you!"

As he zips his pants back up she says, "Well done, Ron."

He grins at the nickname. Then says, "Was it boob-worthy?"

She thinks it over. "Yeah. It was a good interlude. Quite a brave gesture, actually." She takes his hand, places it on her boob. When he squeezes it she yelps and backs away. "Jesus, Ron! It's not a peach, okay?"

As his face reddens, she immediately regrets her comment and moves toward him, saying, "Sorry. It's just me. I'm sure most girls are far less sensitive. Let's try it again with the other one, and I'll show you exactly how I like it."

This time Colin and Henry move close and study the demonstration like she's a magician revealing the world's greatest magic trick. it only lasts a few seconds, but all three commit the lesson to memory. Then Lindy says, "Lay your wardrobes out in your trunks so I can see them."

They go to their cars, pull their wardrobes from their bags. She approaches Ron and says, "Turn the pockets inside out."

As he does, two index cards fall out of his pants pocket.

"What the fuck is that?"

Ronald picks them up. "One's a cue card with dialogue notes. The other's the date, time, and location for today's meeting."

"Are you *insane*? What kind of home invader would you be in real life?"

"First of all, I'm an actor, not a home invader. If we ever get to the part where we're actually on camera, I wouldn't bring the cards."

"Good to hear. Hand them over."

He gives her the address card immediately, but takes one last look at the cue card before she snatches it from his hand.

"C'mon guys, time's running out. We need to get better."

She checks their outfits, has Colin disburse the guns and handcuffs and makes sure their throwaway phones are charged. Then she says, "Ron, as the robbery winds down you'll leave ten minutes early, fetch your car from McDonalds, drive it to the front of my parent's house, and park with the doors unlocked and the motor running. Colin and Henry will finish up, run to the car, and you'll drive to the airport going no faster than the speed limit. From here on out, we're not going to break character. You're home invaders. This afternoon you're gonna lay low, and tonight you're gonna terrify my parents."

"But your parents," Ron says. "They're gonna *know*, right?"

All three men look at Lindy as she says, "No Ron. They're not gonna have the slightest idea. You're literally gonna scare the shit out of them. That's the only way to see how well you've learned your roles. You'll be playing off their authentic responses."

"But—"

"Don't worry. Even though I'll remain in character, I'll be there to manage things. I'll make sure nothing goes wrong."

Colin grins. "I love it."

"Me too," Henry says.

Lindy looks at Ron. "Have I misjudged you?"

He bites his lip. "What if your dad has a gun, or suffers a heart attack or something?"

"How many times have we rehearsed all the possible outcomes?"

"A million."

"So what am I missing? It's not like the whole mission's on your shoulders. You don't even have a *speaking* role! All you have to do is stand there, looking stupid, while everyone else does the work. Then you fetch the car. What's the problem?"

"What you're suggesting...it's real life."

Her eyes blaze with anger. "I'm not *suggesting* anything, Ronald. This is what we're doing. And either you're in or you're not. Which is it?"

In a very quiet voice he says, "I'm in."

"You're certain?"

He nods.

Chapter 49

AFTER SHE POINTS out her house, and McDonalds, she tells them to go have fun, and she'll see them at ten p.m., which is roughly five hours. Then she heads to Jackie Keck's house, visits with Ashley a few minutes, checks the duffel, and transfers the contents to an overnight bag. Then she wipes down the duffel and tells Bill to ditch it in a dumpster.

"No problem. What time should we be at your place tonight?"

"Nine. Have you been practicing?"

"Yeah. Wait. Are we doing the same script as last time?"

"Are you fucking with me?"

Jackie laughs. "Yeah. We practiced. Want to run through it?"

"Maybe we should."

Bill says, "Around ten tonight we're going to argue about how you failed out of college, and how I'm paying all this money for an apartment in Dallas. You don't have a job and now you don't even want to go to Dallas, right?"

Lindy gives a sigh of relief. "Thank you. You had me scared for a moment."

Jackie says, "Like last time we stay in character after the robbers leave, in case one of them hangs around outside the bedroom closet.

We pretend we're a family in crisis, and we just dodged a bullet. We're emotionally spent, and we realize the most important thing is family, and we make nice."

"Our group hug moment," Bill says.

"Yeah," Lindy says. "Except this time you're not gonna grab my boobs in the dark."

"*What?*"

"That was me," Jackie says, with a laugh. "Just having a little fun. Don't be so serious."

Lindy frowns, thinking, *No bigger than my boobs are, they get a lot of attention.*

Bill says, "Do I need to get the knife?"

"What do you mean?"

"Is someone coming to the door afterward like last time? The alleged neighbor, walking a dog?"

"No. We left that part out."

"But we still get paid the same, right?"

"Yes."

"Excellent."

"So we're set?"

He looks at Jackie. She nods.

Lindy rolls the overnighter to her car and lifts it into her trunk. Then she drives to the Brown Hotel, parks in the parking garage, enters on the second floor, takes the elevator to the fourth floor. Now, standing in front of Room 412, the door opens before she even knocks, and Joe Wilcox hurries her inside.

"Where have you *been?* I told Kim I'd be home by ten."

Some things never change.

"Sorry," Lindy says. "It was unavoidable. I had customers at the store. But we've still got a good two hours. No. Let me rephrase that: we've got time for a *great* two hours."

As she gives him a full-body hug she glances over his shoulder at the large stack of fifties on the desktop, and smiles. Since he brought the full thousand, there's no need to punish him. As if on cue, he breaks the hug and says, "I brought you a little something."

Lindy bats her eyes. "What do you mean?"

He smiles and points to the cash and says, "Don't be upset. It's just a little something to help with your expenses."

She purses her lips almost to a pout, then slowly breaks into a smile and says, "How could I possibly be angry with you? You've always taken such good care of me!" She kisses him, then says, "And now, I'm gonna take really good care of you!"

After she does, she checks her phone and finds it's only seven-fifteen, which means Joe won't be leaving for forty-five minutes, which means he'll expect her to lie in bed with him and cuddle and listen to his nonstop bullshit about how horribly Kim treats him, and how she and Terri don't appreciate him. Though everything he'll say is true, it won't make his whining any more palatable. Still, it's a thousand bucks for two hours' work, tax free. And there's a side benefit that can't be underestimated: every time she fucks Joe it's another nail in his spoiled, bitchy daughter's heart, even as Lindy removes another thousand bucks from the family kitty that Terri will someday hear about. Even more importantly: since Joe has a heart condition and he's not likely to make it to retirement age, Lindy's taking precious afternoons of Joe's life that Terri will never be able to have.

"I need to pee," Lindy says, padding to the bathroom. She locks herself inside and uses the time to get her head back in the game. Should she exit the bathroom with a sad look? As in, *I'm so sad because you don't have time to cuddle with me.*

She plays it in her mind and decides he'll insist on cuddling whether she comes out happy or sad. Therefore, no sense in being a downer. Fantasy is everything when it comes to affairs: guys like Joe want someone younger and prettier than he could ever get in the real world. And this young, hot babe will not only be perpetually perky, dying to spend every last minute in his arms, but she'll also feed his fantasy that she'd love nothing more than to move in with him permanently, and give him sex for hours every day. After all, she's so *into* him, how could she not?

Lindy sighs. She's tired, and has a long night ahead of her. Ordinarily she would have put him off for calling last-minute on such an important afternoon, but Joe's her steadiest source of income, and she can't take the chance he might call someone else. She doubts he'd find anyone who could match her looks *and* play the girlfriend role as well as she does, but he could certainly find someone adorable who lives a lot closer. It's quite a tribute to her acting ability that Joe's willing and eager to bypass dozens of quality hookers in his home town and drive four hours round-trip to spend time with her.

In the end, this is what motivates her to burst from the bathroom with boundless energy and a dazzling smile. It's what allows her to utter the absurd sentence: "I know it's getting late, handsome, but don't you *dare* try to leave without giving me some serious cuddling."

"Well...maybe just a little," he says.

"*Really? Omigod!* I'm so *excited!*"

He smiles.

Chapter 50

FOR THE PAST four weeks Detective Steve Emmert has had a standing arrangement with the local car rental agencies to notify him if a young lady named Lindy Bissel attempts to rent a car. The agencies have been instructed not to let her drive any car off the lot until Emmert says it's okay. He figured none of them would follow through, so imagine his surprise when he got the call this morning that Lindy called Target Rent-A-Car to reserve a midsize.

"When is she picking it up?"

"Three p.m."

"Thanks. Let her have the car."

When Lindy's shuttle arrives at the Rent-A-Car lot, Detectives Emmert and Wilson watch her step out wearing black yoga pants and a white, sleeveless tank whose open sides are designed to show off a coral-colored jog bra. As she locates her rental car, Wilson laughs and says, "Tongue back in your head, Steve."

Emmert says, "Can't do it. Unlike you, I'm single. I still get to dream."

"We can all dream."

Lindy climbs in her car, adjusts her seat and side mirrors.

Emmert says, "Have you ever in your life wondered what it would be like to wake up next to a woman who looks like that?"

"No."

"Seriously? Never?"

"Nope. I'm more interested in wondering what it would be like to fuck her."

They laugh.

"How often do you have these thoughts, John?"

"Every time I see Lindy Bissel."

She drives off the lot and, to Emmert and Wilson's shock, drives right back to the airport, where she drives up the ramp and turns into the top floor of the short-term parking garage.

Emmert says, "Are you seeing this? What the fuck is she up to?"

"Maybe she's having an affair with a married guy who's flying into town to meet her. She picks him up in a rental car, gives him the keys, and when his wife checks his credit cards she's none the wiser."

Emmert says, "Could be that. But it could also be related to the trip she made to Cincinnati last week. I can't follow her into short-term without being detected. What should I do?"

"There's only one exit ramp, so make a loop around the parking garage, enter short-term on the ground floor and position your car where we can see her come down the ramp."

They find the perfect observation point, then park the car and roll down the windows. Emmert says, "How big you think her tits are?"

"This again?"

"Indulge me."

"34-C."

"What's her best feature: face or body?"

"Both."

"Yeah. I agree."

"Steve?"

"Yeah?"

"That look on your face is creeping me out."

"What would you rather talk about?"

"Our fucking pensions."

"Don't get me started."

Twenty-five minutes later Lindy drives her rental down the exit ramp, followed by a navy blue Taurus with Ohio plates. Emmert exits the garage and falls in line behind the Taurus.

The cost of short-term parking under an hour is just a dollar. They watch her pay it, then see her drive about fifty yards before slowing her car to a crawl, as if waiting for someone.

"You think she made us?" Emmert says.

"No. We're pretty well hidden by the Taurus."

"Keep an eye on her while I pay the ticket."

"No problem. She just came to a dead stop."

After the driver of the Taurus pays his ticket, Emmert pulls forward and holds his ticket out for the attendant.

"Make it quick," Wilson says. "She's moving."

Emmert pays the ticket and speeds out of the toll area.

"She's getting on 264 East," Wilson says.

Emmert speeds up, merges onto the freeway, then switches lanes and finds himself behind Lindy and the Taurus. Four miles later Wilson says, "You see that?"

"What?"

"The Taurus is following her."

"You sure?"

"When we got on the freeway, she got in the middle lane. The Taurus switched lanes and pulled in behind her. Just now she got in the right lane, and the Taurus followed."

"Maybe they're both getting off at the same place."

A few miles later, Lindy exits the freeway and turns right on Westport Road. The Taurus follows, as does Emmert. Five miles later she turns left on Stonehurst and the Taurus follows.

"She's going home," Wilson says.

"Why?"

"How the fuck should *I* know?"

"I mean, why leave home in your car, drive to the airport to rent a car, only to drive the rental car back home?"

"I've got no answer for that."

Lindy surprises them by driving past her house. They follow her and the Taurus to McDonald's, then watch both cars circle the restaurant and head back the way they came. If Emmert pulls into McDonald's Lindy is almost certain to recognize him. So he continues driving straight.

"What now?" Wilson says.

"Time to get fancy."

"What's that mean?"

"We turn right twice and hope for the best."

Luckily, it works. As they make their second turn they see Lindy and the Taurus zipping through the neighborhood intersection a block away. Emmert turns the corner and follows them past Lindy's house and all the way back to Westport Road.

"If they split up," Emmert says, "who do we follow?"

"The Taurus."

Sure enough, when they get to Westport Road, the cars turn in opposite directions. Emmert and Wilson follow the Taurus to a movie theater and observe three men, approximately twenty years old, exit the car, walk to the ticket window, and purchase tickets. Completely baffled, the detectives park near the car. After an hour, Emmert says, "I need to stretch out. You feel like driving?"

"Sure."

They switch seats, Emmert reclines his and takes a nap. An hour later, Wilson wakes him up and they watch the three men leave the theater, get back in their car, and drive to Reggie's Diner, where they wait fifteen minutes for a table before they're finally seated.

While the three guys enjoy a leisurely dinner, both detectives take the opportunity to enter the diner at different times to use the restroom. When Wilson comes out he's carrying soft drinks. By then, it's dark outside. Then Emmert goes in and comes out with a couple of burgers. At approximately nine-forty-five the three young men pay their tab in cash, climb in the Taurus, and drive back to Stonehurst, with Wilson following at a safe distance.

As they approach Lindy's house Wilson spies the rental car parked on the street.

"Lindy's home," he says.

At that very moment the Taurus slows nearly to a stop in front of Lindy's house.

Emmert says, "I don't like the look of that."

"They're up to something." Wilson agrees.

Now, at McDonalds, they watch the men enter the restroom carrying duffels. When they come out they're dressed in black. They put the duffels in the trunk and don backpacks.

"What do you want to do?" Emmert says.

"Follow them."

They hang back, watch the men walk out the parking lot.

"If they turn left, they're going to Lindy's," Wilson says.

"I agree."

The men turn left.

Wilson drives past them.

Emmert says, "Where are you going?"

"Somewhere we can watch Lindy's front door." Then he laughs.

"You think this is *funny?*"

"I think it's hilarious. Don't you get it? She's back in business."

"What are you talking about?"

"There were three men in the original gang: Ian Keller and the Foster twins. Three men, dressed in black. With ski masks."

"Keller said they parked in Lindy's driveway. Not McDonald's."

"So she changed things up this time. Made some refinements."

"I don't buy it."

"C'mon, Steve, it's obvious: Keller said the first robbery was a dry run. She wanted to see how the guys would respond."

Emmert says, "The parents knew nothing about it. They passed the polygraph."

"She's an actress, right?"

"So?"

"Her parents said they were out of town that night."

"And they were. We checked, remember?"

"Like it was yesterday. But what if Lindy hired actors to play her parents that night?"

Emmert mulls it over. "Nancy and Ryan claimed nothing was missing. And they passed the polygraph on it."

"What if Lindy planted the loot for Ian Keller to steal?"

"Here they come," Emmert says, as the men come into view.

"This should be fun."

Emmert says, "What if everything you said is true, but these guys heard the story from Ian and the twins? What if these guys are copycats? Real home invaders who decided to recreate the robbery?"

Wilson rubs his face, thinking about it.

Emmert says, "They've got three backpacks. If they're copycats they'll have automatic weapons. We should call for backup."

Wilson says, "No need. I was right the first time. This is Lindy, back in business with a new gang. I'll lay you ten to one her parents are out of town again, and she's got two actors posing as her parents. That's why Keller and Foster couldn't identify their photos. But I'll bet you any amount of money they'd be able to identify the couple in Lindy's house right now."

"You're basing all this on what, exactly?"

"She stopped her car."

"What do you mean?"

"At the airport. After paying her parking ticket she stopped the car to wait for them. Then she had them follow her to her house, then to McDonald's. She was probably on the phone the whole time, saying, 'that's my house on the left. There's the McDonald's where you'll park your car and change your clothes. Here's the route you'll take when you walk to my house.'"

"What if you're wrong?"

"No way. She's breaking in a new crew. Staging the whole thing."

"But the guys think it's real?"

"Exactly."

"If you're wrong, people could die."

"If that happens, our story is we got here too late. Deal?"

When Emmert fails to respond he says, "Do I need to remind you what they said at the meeting last week? That after all these years of paying into the system our pensions are virtually worthless?"

"No. Aside from Lindy Bissel, that's *all* I think about. We put our asses on the line day and night for fifteen years, for what? I lost my *wife* over this fucking job! Then I take a chance on a woman like Mimi Johnson, thinking I'm finally going to have a chance at a decent retirement, and...those *motherfuckers*!"

They watch the men put on ski masks.

"I broke up with Mimi," he says.

"Sorry, Buddy. I truly am. But what I need to know is, if this thing goes south on us tonight, are you going to back up my story?"

"Always," Emmert says.

One man removes what looks like an automatic weapon from his backpack.

"Showtime," Wilson says.

And then something completely unexpected happens.

Chapter 51

DETECTIVE EMMERT'S PHONE rings.

Wilson says, "Are you *shitting* me? Your phone just lit us up like Christmas!"

"Sorry."

As he scrambles to shut it off he realizes it's Lindy Bissel. He puts the phone on speaker and answers with "Yeah?"

"Hi Detective. It's Lindy."

"What's up, Lindy?"

She laughs. "I was gonna ask you and Detective Wilson the same question."

Wilson says, "Tell us about the guys on your doorstep. The ones wearing ski masks."

"Hi Detective. What would you like to know?"

"Are they carrying weapons?"

"Yes."

"Are they loaded?"

She laughs. "You think I'm crazy?"

"Jury's still out."

"Well, I can assure you there are no bullets on this property."

Emmert says, "Not sure we can trust you on that. We'll need to verify."

She sighs. "I knew you were coming, but I was hoping you'd observe and not interrupt."

"We're law enforcement. We need to be free to do our jobs."

"There are no laws being broken tonight."

"I believe you. Except that I've already seen an automatic weapon on your doorstep. That bears looking into."

"That's just Colin. He's got a permit to carry. Please tell me you're not planning to introduce yourselves as detectives."

"Why wouldn't we?"

"It would scare the piss out of my guys."

"What happens when the neighbors call the police?"

"They've already been alerted. They're fine with it."

"That must've been an interesting discussion."

"It was. I'd love to tell you about it, but I'm rather busy at the moment with this home invasion thing."

"So we see."

"How about this: my guys don't know it, but I'm videoing the entire robbery on three cameras. I can patch your phone into the live feed on a split-screen."

"Where are your parents?"

"Out of town."

One of the robbers knocks on the door.

"Please decide quickly!" Lindy says.

The detectives look at each other in the cell phone light. Emmert says, "Give us a sec. I'll call you right back." After hanging up he says, "God, I love her."

Wilson says, "She's something else, all right. Ballsiest chick I ever met. And only what, twenty-two?"

"Yeah." Emmert pauses. "So what do you want to do?"

The man on the doorstep knocks again.

"Personally, I'd like to watch."

"Me too."

Emmert calls Lindy back. "If you're serious, we'd like to take you up on it. What do you need?"

"Nothing. Click on the link I'm sending and wait ten seconds. Sorry, but I don't have time to patch Detective Wilson in."

"No problem. We can share my phone. Good luck!"

"Thanks."

He hangs up.

Wilson says, "Good *luck?*"

Emmert laughs. "What can I tell ya? *I love this girl!*"

"I know you do," Wilson says.

Chapter 52

OVER THE NEXT thirty minutes, while watching all the activity going on inside, John Wilson does a lot of thinking. He watches the one guy leave, sees him return with the Taurus minutes later, sees the other two rush out the door, watches the Taurus pass him at a normal pace.

"What do you think?"

"I can't believe it!" Emmert says. "It was like watching a real burglary! Each guy had a specific role, and they played it perfectly. And the parents: holy shit! As for Lindy, Jesus, John, she was brilliant! A natural!"

"You believe they could pull it off?"

"You mean a real robbery?"

"Yeah."

"Absolutely! In fact, it *has* worked, right? I mean, we could probably put her away for this."

Wilson laughs. "She's playing with us."

"What do you mean?"

"Look."

He points to the people walking toward Lindy's house.

"Who're they?"

"The neighbors. Lindy alerted them, remember?"

"Now that you mention, it, yeah."

"She obviously told them she's filming a scene for a movie. If you try to bust her she'll say she's using all the information we gave her about the gang to make a movie about it."

"Casting herself as the lead."

"Exactly. Can I ask you something?"

"What's that?"

"Is it too late to get back together with Mimi?"

"Yeah. I blamed it on the pension a while ago, but the truth is she was about to break things off anyway. We're both too old and jaded to start over. Why do you ask?"

"Technically, we're off duty. You got a few minutes?"

"Of course. What's up?"

"We need to talk."

"About what?"

"Our futures."

Chapter 53

LINDY BISSEL LOOKS up from her desk to see not one, but two police detectives enter her store.

"Hi guys. Want some coffee?"

"We're good," Wilson says. "Got a few minutes?"

"I do. I'm just editing the videos from last night. Based on what you saw, and your years of experience, do you have any criticisms to offer?"

Emmert says, "Are you serious?"

"Absolutely. If I wind up making this movie, I'd like it to be as authentic as possible."

Wilson says, "In that case I noticed a couple of things: first, I agree you need three men. But you only need two for the home invasion. The driver should be a driver throughout. He should have dropped the others off in front of the house, then parked nearby and listened to the robbery on with his cell phone."

"How would that work?"

"The leader calls the driver before exiting of the car. Then he clips his phone to his belt and keeps the phone on throughout the entire robbery. The driver has an earbud in one ear so he can hear what's going on inside, but he'll also have his window open so he

206

can hear what's happening around him. Ideally, the driver would also have a police scanner. Three guys dressed in black walking a quarter-mile from McDonald's at night is awfully risky."

She nods. "Thank you. Makes sense."

He says, "By extension, when you had the guy leave the robbery to get the car, if the neighbors had called the police, they could have captured the driver, and he'd have no way to alert the others. But if he was in the car the whole time and saw police in the area he could shout into his phone and the leader would hear it."

"Outstanding!" Lindy says.

Emmert says, "You should also use an assortment of fake ID's and driver's licenses and disguises to match them when you rent your cars. It would add an extra layer of security."

She nods. "Makes perfect sense...assuming the girl in the movie knew how to obtain a fake ID and driver's license. Other than stealing one from a girlfriend, of course. Because she'd also need a credit card."

"Once she had the fake ID and driver's license she could easily get a debit card in that person's name. The car rental agencies and hotels would accept that."

"Well, again, that would be great, but if my movie follows that story line, I'd have to know a credible way for my heroine to get the ID and driver's license. And she's the type of girl who has no underworld connections."

He and Wilson look at each other. Then Wilson says, "If you put us on your payroll, that's just one of many ways we could help you."

Lindy arches a brow. "That sounds like a setup. One that could eventually cause an attorney to claim entrapment."

"We're dead serious, Lindy. We want in. Assuming you make it worth our while."

She gives them a look. "Do you have experience in this sort of thing?"

"Not the payola part. We've been clean our entire careers. Then again, we're overworked, underpaid, and—after spending 15 years turning millions of dollars' worth of drugs and cash over to our bosses—had a come-to-Jesus meeting where we learned our police pension has underperformed to the extent we're facing a cat food retirement."

"Why *this*? Most cops supplement their earnings working as security guards or bouncers."

Wilson says, "That's chump change. We've got a lot of catching up to do."

"I understand. But why *me*?"

Emmert says, "You're the most devious, calculating, manipulative person I've ever met."

"Brazen," Wilson says. "Don't forget brazen."

She smiles. "There's a compliment in there somewhere, right?"

"Of the highest sort."

"Apart from the fake ID, how could you help the heroine in my script?"

Wilson smiles. "Can we cut the hypothetical bullshit? We just told you we're going on the take. There's nothing to stop you from being sincere."

"Sorry. Nothing personal, but until I've personally witnessed you committing a crime, like taking a bribe or something, I'll have to talk in hypotheticals. That said, what could two detectives offer my heroine?"

"Our expertise, our connections, and our protection."

"Can you give me specifics?"

"We've talked about the fake identities. That's a biggie, and we can help you and your guys get several. But more importantly, Steve and I love your store. It's the perfect way to move your stolen property. But you can't use it till you put us on your payroll."

"Because you bought into Keller and Foster's story."

He nods.

"Why?"

"You were *too* good. When we interrogate two people separately for hours on end, their stories never match up. But these two had perfectly-matching stories down to the tiniest detail."

"None of which could be proven," Lindy reminds them.

"True. But it was enough to make Steve want to check your records every week."

"Eventually he would have stopped. It's a lot of work, and he would have found nothing because I actually do run an honest business."

"True, but you wouldn't *have* to."

"And it was never your *plan*," Emmert says.

"What makes you so sure?"

"I spoke to your acting teacher."

"What could *he* have possibly told you?"

"He said the idea for the home invasion skit was *yours*. And *you* chose the actors you wanted to work with."

She cocks her head. "That's really good work, Steve. Why didn't you mention this before?"

"I didn't think to call him till this morning."

"I'm surprised Ian and Rayburn never mentioned it."

"They've had a lot on their plate. But let's not get off track. If you put John and me on your payroll, you'll be free to operate out of this incredible store. Otherwise, you'll have to deal with fences, and eventually they'll rat you out."

"Also," Wilson says, "If one of your future victims goes to the police, we'll either get the case or hear about it. We can keep you up-to-date on how the investigation's proceeding and help protect you every step of the way."

"That would be very helpful. Assuming I decide to pursue the business of home invasions."

Wilson frowns. "I really wish you'd drop the pretense."

"It's not a pretense. I'm still trying to decide."

"What's holding you back?"

"It's a tricky business trying to mold these guys into criminals. That said, it'd be a snap if I could tell them I had detectives on the payroll..."

"Unacceptable."

Emmert says, "We trust *you*, not them. If they're caught they'll sell you out in a heartbeat. Your last gang did."

"So it would appear. And since I was publicly accused, and investigated, can you just imagine how much trouble I'd be in if a second gang of home invaders were to accuse me of masterminding their robberies?"

"You'd be toast. Which is why you need our help to keep from getting caught."

Wilson says, "But only you can know about us. Because even if you told your guys you had cops on the payroll, instead of detectives, Internal Affairs will eventually figure out it's us. Bottom line, the crew can't know."

"I understand."

Emmert says, "What would it take to convert these guys?"

"I'm not sure. I'll have to test the waters. We'll have to rob someone simple first."

"One of your contacts?"

"No. A setup. A guaranteed payoff to build their confidence. You know anyone like that?"

"Maybe. But you'd have to do things differently next time around. You'd have to be able to control the guys better."

"No problem. The personnel dynamic of that crew was screwed up from the start."

"Can we assume you learned from those mistakes?"

"Yes."

"What's different?"

"This time I personally casted the actors and made sure they didn't know each other. They're not just from different cities, but different states, as well. I studied their audition tapes, hired them for the roles, taught them the script, and paid them for each study session. From the very start they looked to me as the leader because I'm the one with all the money, experience, and contacts. They trust me...And we've become quite close."

"Intimate?" Wilson says.

"Not yet, but I won't rule it out."

"You'd *sleep* with them?" Emmert says, with the widest eyes she's ever seen on a human's face.

"I'd do whatever it takes to uphold my end of our bargain," Lindy says. "But for now, let's just say they're attracted to me and want to please me."

"And if one of them falls in love or gets jealous like Claiburn did?"

"I'll be able to keep them in line. I could have done it the first time around if the crew hadn't been comprised of brothers and their close friend, and if two of them hadn't tried to cheat me. That's what brought it all to a head. That wouldn't happen the second time around."

Wilson thinks about it, then nods. "I believe you. But I should also point out a big mistake you made the first time around."

"What's that?"

"The attack on Terri Wilcox."

"What about it?"

"That was a huge, unnecessary risk. I can't believe Terri's parents didn't report the burglary after she got hurt. Any idea why they kept quiet?"

"Yes, but I'd rather not say."

"According to Keller and Foster, the attack on Terri was personal. They felt it was payback for something Terri did to you."

Lindy shrugs. "Whatever the reason, I can assure you it will never happen again."

"We don't need to know everything that happened, but we *do* need to know about Terri. Because it's out of character for you, or at least I hope it is."

Lindy nods. "Okay, so Terri Wilcox never knew me, but she got drunk one night and gave my boyfriend Garrett a blow job in the teacher's parking lot, sophomore year. Garrett broke up with me over it saying Terri Wilcox did more to him in two hours than I did in two months."

"So they dated? Terri and Garrett?"

"No. When he called her the next day she claimed she'd never seen him before. She denied it ever happened."

"Maybe it didn't."

"At least three people saw them, including my best friend, who agreed Terri was so drunk she probably didn't remember."

"So years go by and then you punish her? That's a lot of rage over a drunken blow job."

"Are you married, Detective?"

Wilson nods.

"If you caught your wife giving a guy a blow job you might eventually forgive her, but you'd *never* forgive the guy. And if you had a chance to punish him, knowing you wouldn't get caught, you'd probably allow it to happen. Terri sucked Garrett's dick: she's lucky she didn't get her jaw broken. That would be the proper punishment."

"I get that. But you don't strike me as the type of person who'd be that angry over losing an asshole like Garrett."

"It's a long story."

"Summarize it."

"Under normal circumstances, when the president of a sorority gets caught giving drunken blow jobs to strangers in the teacher's parking lot, she loses...*everything*. It would be the biggest story of the year. But Terri always seems to get a free pass, and this was no exception. By the next day no one was even talking about her."

"Why's that?"

"There was another incident that weekend, unrelated to Terri. A sorority girl nearly died in an accident."

"And you knew that girl?"

"Everyone did." Lindy pauses. "Like I said, it's a long story. I lost a boyfriend, Terri paid no price, and she went back to being her daddy's perfect little angel. But after that weekend, *I* changed. I stopped trusting people. I...became a different sort of girl." She locks her eyes on Wilson's and says, "Can we leave it at that?"

He nods.

Emmert says, "Your crew was excessively rough with the Reinhold girl. What happened there?"

"I knew nothing about that till you brought it up at my parent's house. Again, the crew went rogue. I was the outsider and they were close friends and relatives. But it won't happen again. My second crew will look to me, not each other."

"Glad to hear it," Wilson says. "One last thing: how do you find your victims? Keller and Foster said you had hundreds of contacts as a result of being a sorority girl. But we know that's not true. So how did you get the names and addresses?"

Lindy smiles.

Chapter 54

EMMERT SAYS, "WE don't care where your victims come from. We just want reassurance there are enough of them to make it worth our while."

"Like you said, there are hundreds."

"How's that possible?"

"They come from three sources. The first is sorority-based, and revolves around a young lady who suffers from agoraphobia and extreme social anxiety due to being disfigured in a car wreck."

Wilson arches an eyebrow, but says nothing.

Lindy continues: "The second is the list of men the sorority sisters dated. And the third is derived from something I can't reveal, but it has to do with my extracurricular activities while a student at IU. Is it time to talk about your remuneration?"

"Yes. It would have to be cash only, in advance, and can't be tied in any way to the sale of stolen goods."

"In other words, you'd collect a flat fee on a regular basis."

"That's correct."

"How much?"

They look at each other.

"Twenty-five hundred a month. Each."

"*Each?* That's twice my rent! You're crazy!"

"You made $120,000 from one job alone."

"Split four ways. And that was an exception. And sure, I could sell certain stolen items in my store, but the only way to safely sell jewelry is by the stone, without the settings. We're talking twenty cents on the dollar for the jewelry."

Wilson says, "I think you're underestimating the market, but it doesn't matter. You know our participation's worth twice what we're asking, and you can't sell anything without our help."

"When would it start?"

"Immediately."

"What keeps you from increasing the price as we move forward?"

"If you're doing extremely well one year, we'd expect a small increase the next."

"How small?"

"Five hundred a month. Each."

"For that kind of money you'd have to help me with the first victim. Someone local. A slam-dunk."

"How much would your gang have to score?"

"At least fifty grand."

Wilson shakes his head. "We don't know those sorts of people."

Emmert says, "I do."

Wilson gives him a look. Then grins. "Alex Abs?"

"The same."

Chapter 55

"ALEX ABS", EMMERT explains, "is the guy my wife ran off with."

"Let me guess," Lindy says. "They met at the gym."

"Exactly. Except he *owns* the gym."

"I like it. Tell me more."

"His house is upper-middle class, he doesn't appear to own any firearms, and during the week it's just him and Dolly in the house. Every other weekend, his two kids show up."

"How successful is the gym?"

"I expect it turns a profit. But from what I gather his real money comes from selling steroids and possibly drugs."

"Is this guy a muscle head? Is he likely to beat the shit out of my guys?"

"It's not going to matter because your guys are going to break in when Dolly's alone."

"Because he'll be at the gym?"

"Exactly."

"What are the guys likely to find there?"

"Drugs and cash."

"Jewelry?"

"Not so much."

"I don't deal in drugs."

"I expect the cash will be substantial."

"Why's that?"

"Because in one of our arguments Dolly said, 'Alex keeps more money in his safe than you made last year. *Before* taxes!'"

"Since you brought it up, how much *did* you make last year?"

"Sixty-eight thousand, much of which goes to her."

"Would Dolly know the combination to his safe?"

"Possibly. But if not, your guys would have hours to break it open."

"So she's home all day?"

"When she isn't shopping or working out."

"What if there's a silent alarm?"

"Not likely, because if the police showed up he'd have to show the source of the cash. It would be proof he's selling drugs. If this sounds good to you, we can sit down and I can give you all the details."

"What time does Alex leave for work?"

"I'm not sure, but I know it's early. Probably eight or nine."

"I'll check it out for a few days to learn the routine. We'll want to go in shortly after he leaves."

"Why not the afternoon?"

"Being alone during the day, Dolly's probably got friends who come over to visit. If they do they'll probably come in the afternoon."

"She's more likely to meet her friends for lunch."

"Even so, if she's got lunch plans my guys wouldn't have all day to break open a safe."

"True, but I doubt it's a big safe. Probably just in the wall. Might even be something they can pick up and take with them."

"Is Dolly on Facebook?"

"Yeah."

"I'll want that info, and any other social media details you can give me."

"Why?"

"It'll help me build a profile."

He looks at Wilson. No words are exchanged, but they're impressed.

"No problem," Emmert says.

"So I'll want that, and her cell phone number, and date of birth, and I'll want to know how long she's been living there, and which cars they drive, and any other information you can give me."

"Like what?"

"Like do they have a dog? If so, could he be inside?"

"He has a dog, but he takes it to the gym."

"All day?"

"That's my understanding."

"I'll probably use two cars and have Ronald, the driver, follow Alex to the gym and stay there to make sure he stays put."

"Good idea."

"Does Dolly sleep in late?"

"Always."

"So she might not answer the door."

"True."

"You'll need to call her."

"What do you mean?"

"Before the break-in, you'll call her, talk to her about whatever: you still love her, you miss her, you want her back, or maybe she charged something to your credit card or maybe you need to let her know you're gonna be late this month with the check. I don't know. Be creative. Just keep her on the phone."

"Why?"

"So she'll be awake when the guys ring the doorbell, and won't be able to call Alex to ask if he's expecting a plumber."

"You've got a van?"

"How else can I pick stuff up and haul it to storage?"

He smiles.

After Emmert and Wilson leave, Lindy shuts off her recorder and replays their conversation to make sure she's got them on tape offering to take money in return for looking the other way. Then she calls Ronald and says, "I'd like to talk to you today. Are you available?"

"Sure. What time?"

"I'd like you to meet me halfway. You think you can be in Carrollton in two hours?"

"Yeah. It's just forty-five minutes from my house."

"There's a KFC there. Meet me in the parking lot."

"No problem. What will you be driving?"

"My van."

Two hours later, he sees her enter the parking lot, walks over, climbs in, saying, "Last night was fantastic!"

"I agree."

"Did we do as well as I think?"

"Even better."

"You still think we can sell the script?"

"I don't know. Can I ask you something?"

"Of course."

"Do you like me?"

"What?"

"Do you *like* me?"

"*God* yes!"

"Do you *trust* me?"

"Of course."

"How much?"

"What's wrong?"

"Nothing. It's a simple question."

"I trust you completely. What's going on?"

"You guys were incredible last night. Totally believable. You could have pulled off an actual home invasion."

"Well, I don't know about that. I mean, when you told me your parents weren't gonna know about it I nearly shit my pants. I don't think I could have done it if you weren't there."

"I guarantee you could."

"I don't know. I doubt it."

"What's your financial situation?"

"You asked me that the first day you called. Nothing's changed. It's awful. I live with my *parents*! The only money I ever made in any job in my life is what you paid me."

"What about your dating life?"

"I do okay."

She looks at him. "Tell me the truth, Ron. No bullshit. I won't tell the guys."

He frowns. "You'll laugh."

"I would never."

He bites his lip. As he thinks about what to say his face turns bright red.

"Spill it, Ron. I have a reason for asking."

"I've...uh...I've never...you know."

"Never had sex with a girl?"

He shakes his head.

"How far have you gotten?"

"Not very far."

"Maybe we can change that."

"What do you mean?"

"Let's climb in the back a minute."

"*What?*"

She points to the back of the van, where she's placed a mattress.

"Are you serious?"

"I'm not offering intercourse," she says. "But I'd like to get to know you better."

"How much better?"

She shows him a wicked smile. "A lot."

Chapter 56

AFTER TAKING RON'S experience level to a higher place than it's ever been with hands other than his, she hands him a towel. When he apologizes for exploding so quickly she says, "Don't say that."

"But it's true. I only lasted twenty seconds."

"I would have been insulted if you lasted longer. I really enjoyed touching you like that. Can you keep a secret?"

"Of course."

"We're gonna do it."

"We are?"

She laughs. "Not *that*! I mean, not today, anyway. I was talking about me and the other guys."

"What do you mean?"

"We're gonna rob a house." She leans closer, nibbles his ear, whispers: "For real!"

"*What?*"

"You want to join us?"

"No!"

She shows him a hurt look. "Really? You don't want to be part of my group?"

"Not to...I mean...you're not being serious!"

"I am."

"You'll get caught. You'll go to jail."

"We won't get caught. I guarantee it."

"What about the movie?"

"There *is* no movie, Ron. This whole thing was a training exercise."

It takes a minute to sink in. By then they're sitting in the front seats. Ron says, "Lindy, listen to me: there's a *huge* difference between acting out a home invasion and actually doing it. You have no idea how scary it is. Even though I knew it was fake, my knees were shaking the whole time."

"This is probably a good time to tell you I've changed your part. You're only gonna be driving, and nothing else. You'll never even have to enter a house. For you there'd be no guns, no confrontation."

"What do you mean?"

She explains how he'll drive the car to the homes, drop the guys off, keep watch in the neighborhood with his phone on so he can listen as the robbery takes place. "Plus, you're gonna have a police scanner!"

"Still," he says, "this is crazy. The guys are actors, not criminals. You can't predict what might happen during a home invasion."

"I most certainly *can* predict it, Ron. I know all there is to know about it."

"Research isn't the same as actual experience, Lindy."

"This isn't my first rodeo."

He stares into her eyes. "What do you mean?"

"I'm twenty-two years old, fresh out of college. I own two vehicles and a business. Later this year I'll have enough money to pay cash for my own house. Want to know how I finance this lifestyle? I rob houses."

His jaw drops.

"I've never been caught," she says, "and I've been passing this knowledge on to you and the guys since day one. That's how I know everything they're going to encounter inside the homes. I research the victims meticulously. In some cases, I even know the interior layout and where they keep the money. So that's one reason we won't get caught. And the second is I've got two police detectives on my payroll."

"Bullshit!"

"It's true. They were watching you from the street last night. And this morning we met and they graded your performance. By the way, they gave all three of you a perfect score."

Ron shakes his head. "You're fucking with me." He looks around. "You've got a camera hidden in here somewhere, right?"

"Nope. It's just you and me and the secret I'm about to tell you."

"What's that?"

"The secret of what turns me on. Do you care?"

He nods.

"Bravery. I've put together a team, Ron, and I consider you an integral part. I want us to be tight and do things together. And some of those things will be sexual. You and I won't be exclusive, so you can't get all weird and jealous, but you and the guys will be out there for me, and I'm going to reward you for it. So anyway, Colin and Henry are gonna do this whether you're in or not, because I can sure as hell drive the car myself, if need be. In fact, I'll look forward to it. But you're my guy, Ron. You're the one I chose for the part. And I'd like you to get rich with us."

"It's...I mean...thank you, but it's—"

"Ron."

"What?"

"Ever seen one of these?"

She slides her jeans and panties down to her knees and points to her vertical smile. As his eyes bug out of his head she says, "By next week, this can be yours, but you have to decide right now: are you gonna drive the car for us Friday night and collect $5,000 for an hour's work, or is this the last time I'm ever gonna see you?"

Chapter 57

WITH HER DRIVER secured, Lindy drives to Indianapolis and charms Colin into starting his life of crime. Then it's back to Louisville for a few hours' sleep, and the following day she drives to Nashville and gets Henry on board. As expected, Colin and Henry were easier to convince than Ron, though she wasn't sure if it was her robbery experience, her detectives on payroll, the promise of making at least $5,000, or the blow jobs that had the biggest effect on their decisions.

Now, back in Louisville, she takes her overnight bag, minus half the contents, to Jackie and Bill's house.

"I thought you gave up on us," Jackie says.

"I've just been swamped, but it's all good. So anyway, here's my overnight bag. Inside there are 25 Morgan silver dollars and 10 Krugerrands. The boys are gonna rob your home Friday night and this is what your actor friends are gonna turn over to them."

"Just to clarify, we're getting $5,000 for this, right?"

"Yes." She hands her an envelope and says, "In advance."

"And our actors?"

"A thousand each."

"And you said you'd be here?"

"Yes. The storyline is, I'm friends with your daughter, and I'm here, visiting, talking to Ashley's parents, who'll be played by actors, and suddenly the doorbell rings, and it's a robbery."

"I'm still not sure how you plan to keep them from coming upstairs. The deal was, you could use our home, but we'll be upstairs with Ashley the whole time."

"I told the guys Ashley's a paraplegic, so she's no threat. They've been told not to go upstairs for any reason, and of course, I'll be here to control the situation. They think I'm helping them rob my friend's parents. I told them about your coin collection, and I'll give you $880 that the woman playing you can sprinkle in two or three locations. She should put a few bucks in your cars, as well."

Jackie nods.

"Here's how it'll go down: I'll be talking to the mom and dad when they knock on the door. I'll open the door and the guys will force me into your kitchen. One guy will hold an unloaded gun on me and the dad, and the mom will lead the other guy around the house to get the coins and cash. They'll be in and out in fifteen minutes, tops."

"I need your word they won't disturb Ashley."

"I promise. Don't forget, I love Ashley. I would never do anything to hurt her."

"I know that. But it bears repeating."

Lindy gives her the $880, then leaves.

Chapter 58

IT'S FRIDAY NIGHT, and the Keck robbery goes smooth as silk and the guys are ecstatic. An hour later they meet up in Colin's hotel room, and spend the next two hours talking about it: being actors, they parse every word of dialogue, talk about how scared the dad was, how scared *they* were, and how cooperative the mom was after they threatened to beat her half to death. They gush over Lindy's performance and agree there's no way the parents would ever believe she had anything to do with the robbery. Lindy pulls out her phone and looks up the spot price for Morgans and Krugerrands, and says, "I promised you at least $5,000 for an hour's work. You were there twenty minutes and based on today's price for the coins, we're splitting $32,000. That's $8,000 apiece!"

"What about the detectives?" Ron says.

Lindy casts him a scalding look. "You can *never* mention them again. Not ever!"

"Why?"

"Because their fucking *careers* are on the line! You're not even supposed to *know* about them. That's the deal I made."

"I understand that," he says, defensively. "I'm just wondering how they get paid."

Colin groans.

Lindy says, "You're making me really nervous right now, Ron."

"Why?"

"Because you're asking questions that shouldn't be asked."

Henry says, "Let it go, man. Be happy she's got a deal."

Lindy puts her head in her hands. "I never should've told you guys about the detectives. It's just...I didn't want us to have any secrets. I thought I could trust you."

"Thanks a lot, asshole!" Colin says. "Lindy, he's not gonna say anything. We'll kick the shit out of him if he does."

"No," she says. "I want us all to be close. You can't threaten or hurt each other. If you ever do that, you can't be a part of the team. We have to be like family."

"In my family, Dad beats the piss out of everyone. Including Mom."

"Well, that's dreadful. But we're gonna be a happy family if it kills me. Tell Ron you're sorry for calling him an asshole."

"Sorry, dude."

"And for threatening to kick the shit out of him."

"That too, Colin says. Sorry, man."

They shake hands.

Lindy says, "I'm only gonna say this once, and if anyone ever brings up the detectives again, they're off the team forever. Here's how it works: they don't get a cut of each job. I pay them a flat fee every month, and it's a lot. And yes, in the future we'll set aside a portion from each job to help make the payment. But since this is your first job I decided to give each of you a full split, and I'll donate my part toward their next month's pay. I figure that's the least I can do. That, plus this."

"What?" Henry says.

"After every successful job I'm gonna spend an hour alone with one of you, starting tonight. Who's interested?"

Not surprisingly, three hands go up.

"Good. We'll leave it up to chance. You'll each flip a Morgan dollar and place it in your hand. Odd man out gets me for an hour."

"What's odd man?" Ron says.

Henry rolls his eyes. "Like if there's two heads and one tails, the guy with tails gets Lindy."

"What if all three turn up heads? Or tails?"

They look at Lindy, who says, "You'll keep flipping till someone wins."

It only takes one turn.

Henry wins.

After telling Colin and Ron not to pout and that it will be between the two of them next time, she sends them out of the room and tells Henry never to mention whatever happens between them and never to ask what happens between her and the others. "Everyone will have a great time," she says. "But if you guys start talking about me to each other we'll have to stop having these special times. Understood?"

He nods.

She shows him her million-dollar smile. Then says, "Come and get it, cowboy!"

Chapter 59

THE FOLLOWING WEDNESDAY morning a Louisville woman named Dolly Hendricks is arguing with her ex-husband on her cell phone when the doorbell rings. She looks out the window, sees a plumbing van, puts on her house robe, cinches it, and opens her door. One of the plumbers says, "Alex wanted us to check on a leak in the pool house. It'll only take a minute, but we need to shut off the water line in the basement."

She says, "You know where it is?"

"Yes ma'am," Henry says. "We've been coming here for years."

"Okay, then. I'll leave the door unlocked. Come in and out as you need to, and holler when you're done."

She opens the door, but when they come in Colin produces his sub-machine gun. Dolly gasps and drops the phone, but doesn't scream. Henry picks up the phone, terminates the call, and erases it from her phone log. Then he politely asks where she keeps her money. When that request fails to elicit her cooperation, Colin punches her in the face. When she hits the floor he kicks her in the stomach. When that effort falls short, he punches her again.

As it turns out, Alex Abs has a large, stand-alone safe he keeps hidden beneath a tarp in the corner of his bedroom closet. Under threat of removing her liver with a finely-honed 10-inch carbon steel hunting knife, Dolly suddenly remembers the combination. And when she opens the safe, Henry's jaw drops.

Chapter 60

AFTER LOADING THE cash into his backpack, Henry uses Dolly's cell phone to photograph the bricks of heroin, the steroids, the needles, and the plastic bags filled with prescription drugs.

Then he says, "When we leave, your first instinct will be to call Alex to report the burglary, but what you need to do is wait 30 minutes before calling him. And when you do you're gonna tell him to come home. You'll say 'Something terrible has happened,' but you're not gonna tell him what. And when he gets home you won't let him call the police. Because if he does, several things will happen. First, the photos I've taken will be sent to the police and FBI. Second, the photos I'm *about* to take will be released on the Internet, and to every contact you have on your phone and on Facebook. I'm gonna leave the original photos on your phone so you can show them to Alex. I doubt he'll want all his friends and customers to see them. Understand?"

She nods.

"You're probably wondering since the pictures are on *your* phone, how I can send them to all your friends. The answer is I'm sending them from your phone to an anonymous email address that we can access from any phone or computer in the world, at any time. And by the way, you won't be able to use *your* phone history to access the account because it disburses to a dozen untraceable accounts within seconds. But if you or the cops try to access it, *we'll* know, and when that happens, everyone in your world will know. Any questions?"

"What pictures are you planning to take?"

"Glad you asked! I'm gonna take some triple X nude photos. Please remove your robe and underwear, Dolly. If you don't, we'll do it for you."

"No! Please don't do this. My husband won't go to the police. You have my word."

"Your husband's a heroin dealer. There's no telling what he might do. He'll probably hire someone to try to kill us. So either cooperate, or you'll wish you had." When she fails to respond, he says, "If we kill you we'll have nothing to worry about."

"You'll never get away with this. My husband's a police detective."

"Your husband owns a gym."

"I meant my ex-husband. He's a career police detective with the Louisville PD."

"What's his name?"

"Stephen Emmert."

Henry and Colin look at each other. Henry says, "She's probably right. We'll never get away with it. We should kill her."

"No!" she shouts.

But Henry's mind's made up. He finds a pair of gloves in her closet and tells her to put them on. That way, if she tries to scratch him she won't be able to get his DNA under her fingernails. Then he handcuffs her, forces her to lie on her back, and sits on her chest and pins her down while Colin shoves a stuffed animal halfway down her throat. Dolly wants to lash out and scratch the men's eyes out, but the handcuffs and gloves prevent her from doing so. Colin pinches her nostrils shut and waits for her to die.

Then he removes his fingers and says, "This is probably a mistake."

"Why?"

John Locke

"We need permission. I have a 50-50 chance of getting laid tonight, and I don't want to be on our lady's bad side."

"I don't blame you. But we can't exactly call her up."

"Let's take a minute to think it through."

They pull the stuffed animal from Dolly's throat, causing her to retch and gag even worse. Henry laughs. "Did you pick that out on purpose?"

"What?"

"The stuffed animal?"

"Naw, man. There were like 20 in the closet. I just grabbed the first one. Why?"

"It's a fuckin' llama."

"So?"

"We just stuffed it down Dolly's throat! Get it? Dolly Llama?"

Colin's mind is elsewhere. He motions Henry into the next room and says, "You think she was talking about Lindy's detective?"

"Has to be. And Dolly's his ex-wife. He must've given Lindy the contact. He probably wanted to get back at her for marrying this drug dealer."

"Our detective's probably paying this bitch half his salary in alimony."

"Lucky for us, or he might not need the extra money."

"That's my point. If we kill her, he won't have to keep paying alimony. He might not need the extra money we're paying him. And that could be bad for Lindy."

"Shit! I hadn't thought of that! Let's go check on her."

They find Dolly thrashing about in the foyer, twenty feet from the spot where they nearly killed her. Since it's clear she's going to live they take a minute to disable the house phones so she can't call anyone using the land line. By then, Dolly's condition has improved sufficiently for them to get back on script, so they uncuff her, strip her, and Colin asks if he can be the one to—as Lindy said— "Photograph her nudity in graphic detail, being sure to include her face whenever possible."

233

Henry hands him the phone and watches the show with mild interest. Dolly's got a great body for her age, but having seeing Lindy naked just days ago, he eventually grows bored and turns his attention to the photos on the wall, trying not to laugh as Colin attempts to turn the photo session into a major production.

"Now face me," Colin's saying. "Good girl! Now get on your knees and arch your back. Excellent! Now face me and stick your ass in the air toward my partner, and—"

"Holy shit!" Henry yells.

"What?"

"Look at the size of that *asshole!*"

"Fuck *you!*" Dolly yells.

Henry laughs. "Actually, I was referring to your husband's bodybuilding photo. But now that you mention it..."

After Colin photographs her in every pose he can think of, they send copies of the pictures to the anonymous email address. Then they bind Dolly's wrists and ankles with three of Alex's neckties. As they exit the house, they shut off her cell phone and toss it on the roof.

Chapter 61

WHEN DETECTIVE EMMERT shows up at Lindy's store with an expectant look she says, "Have you heard from Dolly?"

"Not a word. How'd it go?"

"Amazing. Did you know Alex Ab's a heroin dealer?"

"You're joking."

"We've got photos of his open safe: bricks of heroin, more than a thousand prescription pain pills, and enough cash to pay both of you three months in advance, plus this."

She hands him an envelope containing $10,000.

"What's this for?"

"It's a bonus for giving us the contact."

"So Dolly knew the combination?"

"She did. But...don't be upset. The guys had to rough her up a bit."

He frowns. "How badly?"

"It'll look worse than it is. She sustained some cuts and bruises. But nothing's broken, far as we know, and no internal injuries."

"How much did your guys take?"

"I'd rather not say."

"Why?"

"Because if you start asking those sorts of questions after every job you might decide to ask for a cut. And we already have a deal in place that made you happy. Not to mention this extra ten grand. We can't get greedy, and neither can you. But I *will* say it was a good day, cash-wise."

"Let me rephrase: what items did you take?"

She gives him a look.

He says, "I'm not asking for specifics, I just need to know before you start selling things on eBay, Amazon, Craig's List, or whatever. I need to make sure no one reported specific burglary items without listing a name."

"The guys took cash only. No drugs, jewelry, or personal items."

"Why not?"

"Not knowing who might come to visit, or when, I gave them a strict time limit of 45 minutes. It took all of that to get into the safe, photograph the contents, and take the steps necessary to keep Dolly and Alex from reporting the crime."

"Can I see the photographs?"

"They're on various websites. I can give you a link to the one that shows the drugs, if you like."

"You're sure it's heroin?"

"No. My guys aren't pros. But *you* might be able to tell from the photographs. By the way, we used Dolly's phone to take the pictures."

"Why?"

"So she could show Alex. I figured that would give him a reason not to report the break in. The guys told Dolly if he reports it, the photos go straight to the police."

He nods. "That takes care of Alex, but not Dolly. If she's severely bruised like you say, her friends are going to ask questions. What keeps her from saying she was robbed? And sure, Alex can talk her out of going to the cops *now*, because of the drugs, but what happens the next time they have a major fight? What keeps her from going to the cops?"

236

"I'd rather not say. But trust me, she's not gonna tell anyone but you what happened."

"Why would she tell me?"

"She's a woman."

"Come again?"

"It means she'll gravitate to her comfort zone. She's been attacked, roughed up, and frightened half to death. She'll probably exaggerate what happened, but she's definitely been through a lot. And she'll tell you her story because you guys have a history, and deep down she thinks you still love her, and care what happens to her. She'll also ask your advice about what she should do, so think that through before you talk to her."

"Did your guys sexually assault her?"

"Not the way you're thinking."

"Dolly has a strained relationship with the truth. If you don't tell me exactly what happened I won't know if she's lying."

"Trust me on this issue. It's better if it's a surprise."

"I'm going to say it a different way: our future association—yours and mine—depends on telling me what happened."

Lindy stares into his eyes until Emmert says, "This is the only exception I'll ever ask. Surely you can understand my situation: it's not just my ex-wife, it's her drug-dealing husband, and I'm the one who called her just prior to the robbery. My ass is literally on the line."

Lindy nods. "Okay, Steve. That's fair. So the guys took photos of the contents of the safe, then they made Dolly remove her clothing and took nude photos of her. The photos have been uploaded to a different site, and will be released to all her friends and associates—some being Alex's customers, which means they whole gym will see them—if she tells anyone."

"Your guys saw her naked?"

"They did."

"You're shitting me."

"I'm protecting you."

"I'll need that website."

"I'm willing to share it, but it'll only piss you off."

"It's not right."

She gives him a look. "Are you *listening* to yourself right now? It's not *right?* We're breaking the *law*, Steve. And don't forget, this was *your* referral, not mine."

"You never said a goddamn thing about taking nude photos of Dolly! It's not right, and you *know* it!"

"Take a breath, Steve."

She waits a few seconds before saying, "Try to remember the thing you and John admire most: that I know how to prevent the victims from reporting their crimes. Think about it: not one victim has ever reported their break in. Even after their *daughters* were assaulted. These photos were necessary. They're insurance. No one is ever gonna see them, but they'll keep Dolly from telling her friends or the police."

She studies his face a moment, then says: "You still love her."

"Not true. But she deserves a degree of dignity."

"You need to let this go, Steve. Put it out of your mind."

"Or what?"

"Or you're gonna start resenting the very men who are funding your retirement."

"Those assholes beat up my wife and stripped her naked!"

"Ex-wife, Steve. The same woman you hated last week when you gave me all her personal information. The one who *divorced* you and ran off with a fucking *drug* dealer. The one to whom you're still paying $2,200 a month in alimony. You know what that means, don't you?"

"Yeah. It means I'm an idiot."

"No. It means you're paying Dolly $2,200 a month to fuck a drug dealer. How often do you think she sucks his cock?"

"*What?*"

"I bet when you first got married she was wild. Probably went down on you every night. But after a few years she gave you less and less, am I right? Take a moment to think about all the things she did for you, back in the day, when you guys were dating."

"Why?"

"Because I guarantee she's doing all those things to *him*. And obviously, a lot *more*."

"What's *that* supposed to mean?"

"I've seen the photos, Steve. And though I generally shy away from criticizing other women's posteriors, I think we can safely assume that Dolly's getting a *lot* of anal action from a guy who's hung like a horse."

"What the hell kind of person *are* you?"

"The kind who knows how to get over a failed romance. You're standing here, pining away...but you're literally paying her to bend over for him. Every month you send her a check so she can buy sexy outfits for the man she loves. And surely you know they're laughing at you. She's complimenting him, telling him what a great lover he is, and don't think she's not putting you down. But if it makes you feel better, Dolly's the exception: trust me, most women don't want a giant horse dick inside them."

Emmert frowns.

Lindy says, "How long did she cheat on you before running off with him?"

He shakes his head.

"You don't know? Well, it doesn't matter. Because in Dolly's eyes you were so low and disgusting that cheating on you wasn't enough. She didn't just want this drug-dealing animal when it was convenient for their schedules, she wanted him 24-7. She couldn't get enough of him. Loves him so much she probably used to stare at her phone, waiting for him to call. And when he did, her heart raced and she was delighted to rush to wherever he was and give him blow jobs and anal sex for *free*. But since you're willing to pay her more than $500 a *week* to suck him off, well hey, she'll take it. And you know why? Because it's another way to get back at you. It's another nail she can pound into your broken, pitiful, miserable heart."

He looks at her for a long time. Then says, "Thanks. I needed that."

"Anytime."

He starts to leave, then says: "If she calls, what should I say?"

"What do you *feel* like saying?"

"After what *you* just said? I'd tell her to fuck off."

Lindy smiles. "That's my detective! That's the guy I admire! The one with balls!"

"Dolly made her bed. She can fucking lie in it."

"Actually, she *shit* her bed, Steve. Just like she shit on you and your marriage. My guys did you a favor. Yes, they humiliated her. But it never would have happened if she'd been faithful. You want my opinion? The bitch deserved a lot worse. She got off lucky. And you know what else? *You* deserve better."

He nods. "You're right. Sorry about all that."

"It's okay, Steve. You're just a bit too close to this victim. That'll change from now on."

"I agree. When's the next job?"

"Soon. I'm working out the final details."

"I believe you."

She watches him walk out the door. When he hesitates on the sidewalk, she looks down and starts working on her computer, so he won't catch her looking and take it as a sign to come back in. Because if there's one thing Lindy knows, it's men. And this guy's within an inch of asking her out. Next time he comes in, he'll hem and haw and finally get up the courage to tell her he can't stop thinking about her. And she'll smile, and act flattered, and give him just enough encouragement to keep him going. Before long he'll start coming in more frequently, and sooner or later she'll start taking him into the back room where one day she'll kiss him, and the next day she'll let him do a little more, and she'll bring him along slowly, but eventually she'll be fucking him regularly just like she's been fucking his partner, John Wilson, for the past eighteen months. Ever since the day she launched her escort website during her junior year at IU.

THE END

Personal Message from John Locke:

If you like my books, you'll LOVE my mailing list! By joining, you'll receive discounts of up to 67% on future eBooks. Plus, you'll be eligible for amazing contests, drawings, and you'll receive immediate notice when my newest books become available!

Click here, and let the fun begin!

Or visit my website, http://www.DonovanCreed.com/

Visit Dani Ripper's website: http://www.daniripper.com/

John Locke

New York Times Best Selling Author

Guinness World Record Holder for eBook Sales!

8th Member of the Kindle Million Sales Club!

(Members include James Patterson, George R.R. Martin, and Lee Child)

*John Locke had 4 of the top 10 eBooks on
Amazon/Kindle at the same time, including #1 and #2!*

...Had 6 of the top 20 books at the same time!

...Had 8 books in the top 43 at the same time!

*...Has written 30 books in five years in six separate genres,
All best-sellers!*

...Has been published throughout the world in numerous languages

by the world's most prestigious publishing houses!

...Winner, Second Act Magazine's Story of the Year!

...Named by Time Magazine as one of the "Stars of the DIY-Publishing Era"

Wall Street Journal: "John Locke (is) transforming the 'book' business"

John Locke

New York Times Best Selling Author
#1 Best Selling Author on Amazon Kindle

Donovan Creed Series:

Lethal People
Lethal Experiment
Saving Rachel
Now & Then
Wish List
A Girl Like You
Vegas Moon
The Love You Crave
Maybe
Callie's Last Dance
Because We Can!
This Means War!

Emmett Love Series:

Follow the Stone
Don't Poke the Bear
Emmett & Gentry
Goodbye, Enorma
Rag Soup
Spider Rain

Dani Ripper Series:

Call Me!
Promise You Won't Tell?
Teacher, Teacher
Don't Tell Presley!
Abbey Rayne

Dr. Gideon Box Series:

Bad Doctor
Box
Outside the Box
Boxed In!

Other:

Kill Jill
Casting Call
When David Died
Sorority Girl

Kindle Worlds:

A Kiss for Luck (Kindle Only)

Non-Fiction:

How I sold 1 Million eBooks in 5 Months!

Made in the USA
Middletown, DE
28 July 2020